Faceless

By

Jeff Monday

Also by the Author:

A Conspiracy of Sins

The Born and the Made

The Story King Chronicles:

Jom

Jom the Light Wielder

Jom the War Bringer

Faceless

By

Jeff Monday

FACELESS

This is a work of fiction. Names, characters, events, and environments are the product of the author's imagination or are used in a fictious manner. Any resemblance to actual persons, living or dead, events, locales, etc., is entirely coincidental.

Copyright © 2021 Jeff Monday

Cover art by Philip Anthony Bailey

For all the voices that aren't heard.

For all the sights that aren't seen.

For all the music that isn't heard.

For all the art that is never experienced.

When Anto was three years old:

Mother swayed Anto gently in her arms. In the other room, Father was pounding together a bed using the wood from Anto's crib. As he hammered, Mother cooed and sang softly, keeping little Anto from crying:

Little pup, little pup

Where have you gone?

The sun is going down

Oh, little pup, come home.

Little kit, little kit

Don't run too far.

The dark things are here

Oh, little kit, come home.

Little one, little one

Don't ask any questions.

The faceless ones are coming

Oh, little one, be silent.

Anto clutched a wooden figurine in his tiny hands and gurgled. He let go of the figure to reach up for Mother's face. The wood hit the floor and, even though Father was in the other room working, heard.

"What was that?"

"Nothing. Anto just dropped Telos."

Father grunted. Even over the hammering, he could be heard muttering.

"...go to the trouble of carving the damned thing...least he could do is hold on to it..."

Mother grimaced but didn't say a word. Instead, she bent over and grabbed the toy from the floor. Seeing it, Anto smiled and reached out.

"Here you go, little one."

Anto clutched the toy to his chest with a happy burp.

"Are you going to grow up big and strong like Telos? Hmm?" Mother cooed to him as the hammered grew louder in the other room. "Are you going to be a great mountain king like Telos?"

Softly, she sang to him, rocking him, keeping him happy so he didn't cry and disturb Father.

When Anto was five years old:

Anto chased the blue flutterby through the yellow grass. He giggled, leaping and twisting, never quite able to catch the bright insect. He chased it all the way to the low stone wall that marked the edge of the field. He blinked back the sudden fat tears welling up in the corner of his eyes as he watched the flutterby erratically move off into the next field, his little hand on the warm smooth stone of the wall.

The sun came out from behind a cloud and brightened the field. He shaded his eyes, keeping the flutterby in sight for as long as he could. Far in the distance, the dark shadow of a tall mountain refused to lighten in the brightness, like a slice of night cutting through the blue of day, something cold and dark stabbing the light.

He sighed as he tracked the insect disappear among the tall grass. With his only playmate gone, Anto turned and trudged back to the house, pretending he didn't hear the yelling coming from within. Every few feet, he looked over his shoulder to see if the flutterby had come back, but it had moved off out of sight among the flowers and leaves. He lingered, dragging his feet as he walked. He smiled in the sun, enjoying the warmth, pretending he was a great and powerful king.

Over the breeze, he heard Mother calling for him. Letting out a dramatic sigh, he whispered farewell to the flutterby and walked home.

When Anto was six years old:

"But I'm not tired!"

Mother glanced across the room, but Father didn't react. She turned back to Anto and shushed him, pushing him back down onto the bed.

"If you don't go to sleep, the Faceless will come for you."

"Who are the Faceless?"

With another glance at Father, she shifted, perching on the edge of the pallet like a nervous bird.

"The Faceless had their faces stolen and they wander the night looking for misbehaving children to take and be their eyes and ears for them."

"But why don't they have faces?"

"Because the Face Stealer took them."

"Why did the Face Stealer take them?"

"Because they asked him a question."

"What was the question?"

"Any question, dear. That is the price for the answer."

"Your face?"

Mother nodded. "Now do you want to get taken by a Faceless?"

"No."

"Then you must go to sleep."

"All right, Mother."

She bent down and kissed him gently on the forehead, then got up and moved away. From his chair across the room, Father grunted but didn't say anything, not even 'good night.'

The wind beat against the wood of the house. Branches scratched at the door. In the corner of the room, Anto huddled under his thin blanket, curled up into a tight ball. He kept his eyes squeezed tight, but his ears couldn't stop hearing the noises from outside. The scratching sounded like a dreadfox trying to get into the house. The wind moaned like a Faceless. Anto shuddered. He made himself as small as possible, not daring to call out. Across the room, he could hear Mother's light snoring and Father's restless tossing and turning. But neither presence gave him comfort.

Anto knew what would happen if he ran to his parents. Father would swat him, irritated that Anto woke him. And Mother would silently plead with Anto to just go back to sleep and not provoke Father anymore.

A shiver ran through his body as the moaning and the scratching peaked just on the other side of the wall from his head. Images filled his brain, scenes of blood, of hordes of monsters tearing at him. He felt something on his leg and almost jumped out of his skin. In that dark storm, a flea's footsteps were as terrifying as a skeletal hand grasping at him.

Squeezing the tears from his eyes, he peeked out from behind the blanket. Shadows moved across the room. The silver light coming from the window and under the door dimmed and brightened as the moon passed behind clouds. The gold gloom from the banked coals in the hearth shifted and glowed. Light without heat. Movement without body. Was that a figure moving across the window? Was that a body sniffing at the door?

He quickly buried his head back under the blanket. He kept his eyes closed but couldn't stop his ears from hearing the sounds around him. Reaching up, he covered his ears with his hands, wishing he couldn't hear the monsters or see their shadowy movements. Shivering from fear and cold, his tears soaked into the blanket. He clutched Telos to his chest, wishing the toy was real and the great mountain king was there to protect him. But he wasn't. Anto was alone in the dark.

When Anto was seven years old:

Anto ran.

Fear, unreasonable, overpowering fear gripped his heart. He knew it was just the other children chasing him. He knew their names. He knew they were just kids, like him.

He ran. They ran after him, moaning and laughing.

"The Faceless are coming for you!"

"Ooooo!"

He knew they were just kids.

But all he could see were Faceless.

"Mother, is the window closed?"

Mother sighed and perched on the edge of the bed. With a sad smile, she reached up and tucked the thin blanket under his chin.

"Yes, dear one. The window is closed."

"The Faceless can't get me?"

She shook her head. "No. The Faceless won't get you. But only if you go to sleep. Remember what I told you?"

He nodded with deep thought. "The Faceless wander the night, looking for bad children who aren't sleeping. They snatch them away to be their eyes and ears."

"That's right. Now go to sleep."

"Yes, mother."

She placed his wooden figurine of Telos beside him on the bed. Instinctively, he wrapped a hand around it, feeling a little better. She smoothed back his hair.

"Good night."

"Good night, mother."

When Anto was eight years old:

"Anto! Anto! Where are you boy?"

Father's harsh voice cut across the autumn wind like a knife.

Anto looked up. The worm in his palm wriggled to the edge of his skin and fell silently back to the cold, wet black dirt. After orientating itself, it squirmed down, back into the darkness and was forgotten.

"Anto!"

Anto stood and brushed off the dirt. He quickly bent down and grabbed the rake that had been lying among the dead leaves he was supposed to be gathering for the fire. He looked down at the woefully small pile at his feet, already feeling the swatting to come.

His sore behind and tears didn't get the chores done any faster. But finally, he finished them all and his father released him to his own devices until it was time for dinner. Anto immediately grabbed his worn wooden figure of Telos and ran into the forest that surrounded the house.

"Die, foul beast!"

Anto struck a branch with Telos. Although battered and splintered from years of play, Telos still could vanquish a foe or two. Anto laughed as the branch broke.

"Another victory for great king Telos!"

Anto raised his arms into the air, Telos triumphant in his grip. Just then, a strong breeze blew through, parting the leaves of the surrounding trees and Anto caught a glimpse of the shadowy spike of rock across the valley. He immediately dropped his arms and quieted. He watched as the leaves fell back into place, obscuring the mountain. Cautiously, he snuck forward, pushing aside the branches until he once more had a clear view.

Far in the distance, it squatted on the horizon, refusing the sunlight. Where its peak touched the clouds, they turned dark and foreboding. Anto shuddered, despite the heat of the afternoon. The peak was evil. Mother said that mountain was the home of the Face Stealer. And that they were always watching. Suddenly the afternoon didn't feel so pleasant. He squeezed the wooden block in his hand, relying on Telos to protect him.

The night was quiet. The winds howled low. By the light of the butter lamp, Anto rubbed a coal of charcoal against a thin piece of slate. His tongue threatened to escape from the corner of his mouth as he concentrated.

"What are you drawing?" Mother asked from her chair, her attention never really straying from her knitting.

"King Telos," Anto replied. "But I can't get the crown right."

"Can't be too hard to draw a crown," his father grunted from the opposite corner of the room.

"Just keep trying," Mother placated, smiling at him though her eyes never looked up. "I'm sure you'll get it."

Anto looked at his drawing, wondering to himself why he couldn't do something as simple as drawing a crown correctly.

When Anto was ten years old:

Greg'r stood over Anto, fists balled and feet planted wide. The smattering of blood on his right knuckles perfectly matched the blood coming out of Anto's nose.

"Not so funny now, are you, runt?"

Anto pinched his nose closed. His eyes were dark, but he kept his mouth closed as he scrambled to his feet.

"Got anything smart to say now?" Greg'r demanded. Behind him, a gaggle of lackeys snickered and pointed. Helpless, Anto watched the wind pick up the pile of papers at his feet and playfully take them away. All his drawings from the last month...gone.

"Well?" Greg'r sneered. But he saw there was no fight in Anto. Nothing to show the others how tough he was. With a casual gob of spit sent into Anto's face, Greg'r turned his back and walked away, leaving Anto alone and bleeding.

Mother, when she saw his injuries, fussed until Father came home.

"Boy needs to learn to defend himself," he told them roughly.

"Those other boys are--"

But Father cut her off with a hard look. Her shoulders dropped in submission. She glanced at Anto, a sad smile on her face. Then she got to her feet and moved to the kitchen to prepare their meal, leaving Anto to tend to his wounds himself. He looked at Father, but he had already forgotten about Anto. Watching Mother's back as she chopped onions, Anto wondered what was happening to his family.

When Anto was twelve years old:

Anto tried not to run ahead of Father. Today was the first time he was allowed to go with Father to Movis, the next village over. Once a moon, Father made the trip to trade for supplies. As they walked the dirt road, Anto's head swiveled from side to side, taking in the new sights. The small fields and stands of trees around his home gave way to large forests, wide rivers and low stone walls that separated fields. Father struck up easy conversations with other travelers on the road. Anto, fascinated by this new, friendly side of Father, didn't notice how Father never introduced him to any of the other travelers. Ignored, unseen by everyone, Anto was thus free to revel in the sights as they walked. He tried to study each and every tree, memorizing the trip for always.

By late morning, they had reached the city. Anto couldn't believe his eyes. Movis was a bustling center of activity. Father led him through the wide streets to the central market, a large open square near the northern wall. Farmers hawked their produce. Cobblers nailed and smithies hammered. Sounds and smells assaulted Anto, nearly overwhelming him. So many people! Anto had never seen more than three or four people together at once before. Only about forty souls lived in his tiny village. But this! He had never realized that there were people all across the countryside. And here they were, going about their business. Anto skipped around, narrowly avoiding the many bodies. Father gruffly pulled him along, muttering to himself. He jerked Anto through the bustle roughly. Near the edge of the market, Father let go of Anto's sleeve and spun him around.

"Wait here. Do not move."

And without another word, Father left him there, disappearing into the crowd to do his business.

Anto stood still for several minutes, watching the bustle around him. His eyes wide, he watched everything at once, trying to absorb all the bustle and chaos of the market. Over there, two hairy men argued over a piece of metal. And over there, a pauper with oozing purple sores begged for money. A group of women walked past, covered in flowing fabric and wildflowers. From the other direction came a priest in a dirty white robe. So many people!

He smiled at the people as they passed by, but no one smiled back. In fact, as he stood there, he soon realized that nobody was paying attention to him at all. His smile faded a little, feeling alone even though he was surrounded by people.

At first, he thought Father would return in a few minutes. But, an hour later, he had not come back. Still, the market was fascinating, and he didn't mind waiting. After another hour though, his legs were tired and sore. He sat on the hard, packed dirt, but was quickly cursed by hurrying people and he had to move several feet towards the wall to avoid getting run over by distracted consumers. He hoped Father wouldn't notice he had moved. Father told him not to move. He looked back at the spot he had been standing at, wondering if he should move back. The hurrying people pushed and shoved and yelled around him though, ignoring him as they went about their business and he decided to stay where he was. Although the activity still held his attention for quite a while, Anto eventually tired of the relentless activity. He looked around for Father, but he was nowhere in sight. Despite his excitement, he felt his eyes grow heavy. Eventually, he dozed off and only woke when, several hours later, Father came to collect him. Father dumped the supplies into Anto's arms and gruffly told him they were leaving.

It was a long walk home. Father was in a foul mood. He had been in his cups, that much was obvious. Any word he directed towards Anto was cruel and biting. Anto kept his eyes on the road ahead, trying to ignore the ache in his arms and in his heart.

When Anto was fourteen years old:

The slap spun him around. Anto clenched his hand into a fist. Father, seeing it, swung again, this time sending Anto to the hard, wooden floor.

"Don't talk back to me, boy," Father snarled.

Anto wiped the dribble of blood from his mouth. He felt a tooth wobble when his tongue slid across it. Eyes full of hatred, he kept his gaze down, knowing that if Father saw that rage, it would be the end of him. Vaguely, he heard Mother sobbing somewhere off to the side.

"Now get up and fetch wood for the hearth."

Even though he was trembling with anger, Anto got to his feet and left the room. He stopped when he was out of sight and listened. He heard the squeak of Father's chair and knew he had sat, his rage spent. Anto nodded grimly. Rage that had been spent on him instead of Mother. Out of the corner of his eye, he saw a worn block of wood on a shelf. Telos. His old toy. Carved by Father for him when he had been born.

The only kindness Father had ever shown him.

He walked over and grabbed the dusty and faded toy from the shelf. Without stopping, he walked outside, adding the toy to the wood for the fire.

When Anto was sixteen years old:

Anto watched the smoke carry his mother's spirit away from the blazing remnants of her body. The funeral pyre burned brightly in the dusky air at the edge of forest. To his right, Father looked like he had swallowed a slice of rotten apple. In one hand, Father held a scrap of Mother's funeral dress. In the other hand he held a bottle. He was paying more attention to the bottle, a fact confirmed by his increasingly loud vulgarities.

"He's in mourning," Lys, the loom-weaver bent close and whispered to Anto. "We all are. He will be better in the morrow."

But Anto knew better. He knew that with the sun would come a fierce round of abuse. His Father knew no other way of expressing himself.

Anto nodded his thanks to Lys, then, with one last look at Mother, turned and walked into the house. He went directly to his room, stuffed his rucksack with a few clothes and an apple from the pantry, and walked away from the only home he had known.

The road took him over the hills just past Father's house.
Even without looking, he knew his small village was soon out of
sight behind him. The dark shadow of Face Stealer Mountain,
however, remained a constant presence, looming over the
countryside. Even after the sun disappeared and the stars came
out, Anto could feel it, somewhere in the darkness.

That first night, he did not make a fire. He didn't want to
chance Father finding him. Before it got too dark, he turned off
the road and pushed his way through the undergrowth until he
found a secluded patch among the trees where he could hunker
down. He wasn't hungry. His grief kept him full. Scooting
between two large boulders, he wrapped his thin cloak around
his shoulders and lay quietly, eyes closed, ears open. Eventually,
the forest sounds lulled him to sleep until the chill of dawn
brought him back to consciousness.

Three villages rose before him and sunk behind as he
continuously moved further and further away. While passing
through one town, he was able to hide away under a filthy
canvas covering baskets of produce in the back of a wagon. It
was half a day before the owners discovered him and chased him
off. Sometimes he followed the roads. Other times he followed
the streams and rivers that crisscrossed the countryside. The days
were hot, the nights were cold, and he didn't have the proper
clothes for either. He lay in ditches, feeling the sweat from the
day slowly freeze against his skin. The only thing that distracted
his thoughts was the rumbling in his stomach. Never more than a
twig of a boy already, he felt his cheeks sink further into his face
and his organs shrink as he wandered the countryside. Thorns
tore his clothing and shredded his skin. At first, he tended his
wounds, but after a few days, there was no point. The blood and
dirt covered him more than fabric after a time, protected him
better than leather. Sadness and fright kept him company as he
wandered.

At one point, he was sure he was going to die, alone in the
wilderness. He even sat down in the dirt, waiting for death to

claim him. But it didn't. After waiting and waiting, he finally got up and continued on. With only the occasional dragonberry or handful of water from a stream to fuel him, he somehow managed to put foot in front of foot, no longer determined to escape, just hoping for an end to the pain, just moving because there was nothing else to do.

It may have been a fortnight, maybe a moon. He didn't really know anymore. He remembered the moon grow full at least once, but the days and nights blurred, and he couldn't remember if it happened more. Some nights, the moon hid behind clouds. Some days, he could barely move, let alone open his eyes. Time didn't matter, was not reliable like it once was.

Weary, half-starved and nearly naked, he stumbled onto a well-worn road, attracted by the sounds of horses and people. He emerged from the underbrush just as a group of travelers were passing.

"Cor! You scared me half to death!"

The shock of people stunned Anto. His mind couldn't react, and his body collapsed. He sat in the dirt, unable to respond. The woman backed up a few steps. Instantly, two large men were at her side.

"Who's this then?"

"I don't know. He just popped out of the bushes."

Anto could feel their eyes on him but had little enough strength to raise his own to meet them.

"On your way," one of the men said, stepping between Anto and the woman, hand clutching a whip hanging from his belt.

Anto struggled to get to his feet. One of the men pushed him and he hit the dirt hard. They moved on, sparing only a wad of spit in his direction. Anto blinked, trying to focus. It had been so long since he'd seen people, he was having difficulty finding his voice. By the time the next group of travelers approached, he was able to croak out a hoarse plea. They ignored him, continuing past with barely a glance.

"Please," he tried again with the next group. "Please. Something to drink? Eat?"

But it was as if he was invisible. Time and time throughout the afternoon, families and merchants sneered at him or ignored him or spat on him. Anto slumped against a tree, too weak to continue. He closed his eyes, hoping death would finally claim him.

The jingle of horse harnesses. The creak of wagon wheels. The laughter of passersby. All the sounds of a well-travelled road washed over him. But all he could focus on was his dry, closed throat and empty stomach. He laughed bitterly, wondering why he ever thought he would be noticed now even though he had never been before.

But just as those thoughts lingered, he heard a wagon stop near him.

"What's this then?" a woman's voice said.

"Looks half-dead," a man's baritone added.

"Jek!" A third voice, this one younger, spoke. "He's barely alive!"

Anto opened an eye. Before him were four people: a man and woman and two younger boys, the youngest about Anto's age by the look of it. The man was standing with hands on hips. The older brother was holding the reins of the horse. The woman rummaged around in a saddlebag. The youngest approached him. Anto closed his eyes, ready for a kick or a wad of spit to hit him. Instead, the stranger squatted down next to him.

"Here."

Anto opened his eyes. The boy was holding out an apple to
him.

"Here," the boy repeated, "eat."

Anto forced his eyes up. In front of him was a kind face.
Fair skin dotted with freckles, dirty blond hair a bit too long.
Oak-colored eyes. The boy smiled kindly.

"I...I have nothing to pay with." The words scrapped Anto's
throat as they came out. Pride, lack of use and thirst made them
jagged.

"Your payment will be the story of how you came to be
here," the boy replied, looking to the woman for agreement.
"When you've rested a bit."

The men grunted but moved off. The woman, after a tut or
two, found a waterskin and passed it to Anto. She nodded to the
back of the wagon.

"May as well hop up," she said matter-of-factly. "Still
another few hours before sundown. We reach Phrable tomorrow.
Don't need you falling and getting trampled before then." Then
she moved off as well.

"Come on," the boy said. Anto unsteadily got to his feet.
The boy led Anto to the back of the wagon and, grasping Anto's
sides, firmly lifted him up onto the lip of the wagon.

"Cor! You're barely heavier than one of Jek's hounds!"

The boy hopped up next to Anto. With a wave to the men
up front, the wagon lurched forward.

"Well, eat up then."

"Thank you..."

"Ven. I'm Ven. Jek is my brother. He's the big 'un with my
da up front. Eon and Mar are my parents. We're heading to

Phrable to sell vegetables and earn a bit of coin doing small repairs and such."

"Thank you, Ven. I'm--"

"Not saying another word until you finish that apple." Ven smiled brightly and pretended to watch the countryside roll past while Anto ate.

The apple led immediately to a contended stupor. It was the first time in days Anto had eaten and his stomach, if not full, was no longer a void filled with nothing but pain. He closed his eyes, rocked by the wagon's movement and soon fell asleep.

"...three oaks, lined up in a row..."

The voice was soft, barely heard over the squeaking of the wheels.

"...next comes the bridge of stone o'er stream so bright..."

He opened his eyes, slowly letting in the bright day.

"...boulder of gray, covered in moss..."

The singing, quiet and soothing, lulled him back to sleep.

When he opened his eyes again, he was nestled among the crates of vegetables. Someone, Ven probably, had tossed a blanket over him. Rubbing his eyes, he looked about. From his vantage, all he could see was the dusty road falling away. The sky was the copper of late afternoon. As he blinked away the sleep, the wagon shuddered to a stop and Ven's smiling face was suddenly in front of him.

"Get up, sleepyhead. You can help me gather wood."

"We're stopping?"

Ven nodded. "Too dangerous to travel at night. We'll reach Phrable early morn."

"Phrable?" Anto scooted forward and carefully climbed out of the wagon. His arms and legs were weak and trembling, but he tried not to let it show. Together, they walked off the road into the underbrush, Ven confident and sure, Anto unsteady but willing.

"Biggest town in the area. You're not from around here, are you?"

Anto shook his head as he picked up sticks. "I don't really know where I am."

"Sounds like you've been having an adventure."

"Not sure I would call it that."

"Well," Ven lightly sprang over a fallen log. "You can regale us all with your grand adventure once we get the fire going and the pot boiling."

They gathered sticks and branches for a few minutes. Anto's brain gradually focused, brushing away the sleep.

"I heard singing earlier. Was that you?"

Looking over, he saw a light blush on Ven's cheeks.

"I...yeah."

"What were you singing?"

"It's nothing."

"Tell me?"

Ven bent over to grab another stick. Straightening up, he shrugged. "It was a songline."

"Songline?"

Ven nodded. "It's like instructions. On where to go."

"I don't understand."

"I come up with a songline for the roads and paths I take. That way I can always find my way again. Just by singing the song. I guess it's my way of remembering my life and journeys."

"That's..."

"Silly, I know." The blush deepened.

"No. I was going to say it's brilliant."

Ven looked at him from the corner of his eye." Really?"

Anto nodded and smiled. "Yeah."

"Thanks."

"How do you remember it all?"

Ven shrugged. "Every time I add a verse, I start at the beginning again. After a while, it sticks in my head."

Anto nodded. "I sing to myself sometimes too."

"What do you sing?"

Anto shrugged. "Mostly just old nursery rhymes my Mother sang to me as a child. I don't really know anything else," he admitted.

"Sing me something."

He felt his cheeks redden. "I don't think so."

"Please?" A wry smile crept across Ven's face, warm and curious.

Anto self-consciously cleared his throat and tried not to look at Ven.

"Little pup, little pup

Where have you gone?

The sun is going down

Oh, little pup, come home."

"I know that one!" Ven laughed. He joined in on the next verse.

"Little kit, little kit

Don't run too far.

The dark things are here

Oh, little kit, come home.

Little one, little one

Don't ask any questions.

The faceless ones are coming

Oh, little one, be silent."

Anto stopped, feeling the exertion on his body. He felt light-headed. And thankful for the kindness Ven and his family was showing him. "I...thank you. For helping me."

"You said that already," Ven pointed out.

"I know. It's just..." But how could he explain to this stranger how overwhelming the simple act of kindness his family had shown him was more than he had ever known? He felt tears forming in his heart, as much from gratitude as self-loathing and bitterness. An apple and a nap. Did it really take so little for him to fall apart? He always believed he was stronger than that. He had survived the scorn and abuse of basically everyone he had ever known. He had known crushing loneliness and refused to give in the blackness that was always threatening to consume him. He had found the strength to walk away from all that, damn the consequences.

After all that, an apple was all it took to finally break him.

His knees gave out and the branches fell with him to the ground. Ven was immediately at his side, cradling his head and telling him everything would be all right. Anto nodded weakly before losing unconsciousness.

When he opened his eyes again, he was lying near a roaring fire. He pushed himself up. A hand steadied him. The woman, Mar, squatted down, handing him a bowl of broth.

"Easy now."

"What...what happened?"

"Took a tumble, you did. Ven ran back here to fetch Eon. They carried you back to camp."

"I'm sorry," Anto mumbled, not meeting her eyes.

"No need for that," she patted his back. "You just eat and get some strength back."

"Thank you."

She waved off the words and stood. As he sipped the broth, he watched the others. Mar tended the pots hanging over the fire while Eon, the father, sat on a log repairing a braided rope. Jek, the older brother, was caring for the horses. Anto didn't see Ven. Every so often, one or another of them glanced in his direction but no one said anything to him. Anto felt his cheeks grow hot. Not from the fire but from embarrassment. He was as helpless as a newborn calf, relying on strangers to tend to him. He realized that his hands were shaking and set the bowl down on the ground. He hung his head, eyes closed, wondering what he was going to do.

"Sleeping again?" a voice next to him asked a minute later.

Anto opened his eyes and saw Ven. He dumped an armful of branches near the fire and smiled at him. Ven took a bowl of broth from his mother and came to sit next to Anto.

"Ma's broth is the best in the five lands," he said, sitting down on the ground with an easy grace.

"It was very good," Anto agreed, although he couldn't really remember tasting it.

"Grab another bowl."

"I couldn't. You all have already been too generous."

He waved it off, just like his mother had moments before.

"Least we can do. You obviously have had a hard time of it lately."

Anto nodded. "You could say that."

Jek took a seat to their right.

"We'd like to hear your story, if you're willing to tell it," he said. His voice was deeper than Ven's and a little warier. Eon and Mar nodded. Soon, everyone was gathered around the fire, all eyes on Anto.

Taking a deep breath, knowing that the only way he could repay their kindness was with his story, he told them of his life. Not everything. He couldn't do that. But the basics. Even still, just the broad strokes of his past were enough to warrant unwanted sympathy. Mar wiped away a stray tear and suddenly needed to busy herself with the cooking pots. He saw a good-hearted pity in their eyes and turned away. He didn't want to be pitied. That was the last thing he needed. But then Ven patted his leg and gave him a smile and he realized that it wasn't pity, it was empathy. Life wasn't easy for anyone, Ven's eyes told him. We understand. The conversation turned to other topics and Anto quietly stood and walked out of range of the firelight, needing a moment to think.

The kindness he was being shown was new. It felt strange. Alien. All his life, he had been a disappointment to his Father, an object to be coddled to his Mother, and a nameless, friendless child to others his age. He didn't know how to react when someone gave him attention, when someone listened to his words. Yet there was something that felt right about this family.

He found a spot at the edge of the trees and stood quiet and still. The surrounding woods were dark and noisy. Rustling, squeaks and growls made it clear that they were far from alone.

"I wouldn't venture too far," Ven said from behind him. "There's dreadfoxes in the area.

"I won't." He hadn't heard the boy approach him but was too exhausted to jump in startlement. Anto listened for him to move off but all he heard were the sounds of the forest. He turned. Ven was standing just behind him.

"I'm sorry. You probably want to be alone," Ven mumbled, realizing he was intruding, turning to leave.

Anto paused only a moment before he spoke without thinking.

"It's all right. I don't mind the company."

"Really?"

Anto tried to smile but it wouldn't come. "Really." There was an easy-goingness to Ven's nature that put him at ease. Anto didn't know if it was his smile, always quick to appear, or his kindness which was continuously evident. All he knew was that he was glad Ven was there.

Ven stepped closed and they stood, shoulder to shoulder, watching the dark forest in silence, listening to the various sounds coming from the darkness. There was a loud snap of a branch and Anto instinctively edged closer to Ven.

"Aren't you worried about what's in there?" Anto asked.

Ven let out a small chuckle. "Only a fool investigates noises in the forest at night," he replied. "Let the forest be and the forest will generally let you be as well."

Eventually, the cool of the night sank through their clothes and they walked back to the fire. Light conversation kept them awake for a bit longer. But Anto's body was exhausted. Soon enough, he was drifting off once more. Once or twice during the night, Anto woke to the sound of a branch breaking or animal huffing in the darkness. But then his eyes fell on the solid shape of Ven's body just an arm's length away. Watching Ven's chest move up and down in easy slumber gave him a feeling of safety and he was lulled back to sleep.

"Do you know what you're going to do next?"

Anto stared at the road under his feet. They were walking behind the wagon. As they neared Phrable, the number of travelers increased around them. Ven and Anto were tasked with keeping an eye on the wagon from behind in case anyone thought about stealing some of their produce. Not that anyone would. It was more of an excuse for them to get to know each other.

"Not really," Anto admitted.

"There's lots of opportunities in Phrable. Maybe you can get on as an apprentice or something."

"Maybe."

"What skills do you have?"

"Not many," Anto admitted. "I mean, I can mend a fence and split logs. But Father never showed me much. Didn't think I could handle it, I guess." Anto tried to keep the bitterness from his voice but didn't really succeed.

They walked in silence for a few moments before Ven spoke up again.

"Pa says you're welcome to come back with us. To the farm."

Anto stopped. Ven did too. Ven looked at Anto. Anto looked anywhere but at Ven.

"I--that's too generous."

Ven shrugged. "Another pair of hands would be welcome around the farm. There's always plenty to do. Pa is willing to put you up for some work."

Anto nodded thoughtfully. His plan upon leaving home had not been more elaborate than: Get Away. Now, after spending too many starving hours wandering the countryside, the thought of a regular meal among good people was very tempting. Having a good friend and loving household was more than tempting; it was everything he had ever wanted growing up.

"Like a farm hand?"

Ven nodded. "Yeah. We've taken them on in the past. Would actually help Pa out 'cause he wouldn't have to look for someone. But I'd be your boss, of course."

Anto looked over and saw a mischievous smile plastered to Ven's face.

"Deal breaker."

Ven laughed. And, for the first time in a very long time, so did Anto.

A few hours later, Anto's senses were overwhelmed by the city. His mind flashed back to when Father had taken him to market that first time years ago. But Phrable was the biggest town he had ever been in by far. Surrounded by high walls, the city was home to thousands of souls. In every direction he looked, people packed its wide streets. Anto and Ven's family had to keep close to the wagon as they slowly maneuvered their way to the market. All around them, people from every land mingled; the cloaked Forest Folk, the quick Prairie Striders, even the haughty Icians of the eastern mountains and the surly canyon Rock Breakers. There were white-robed acolytes of some sort wandering the crowd, proselytizing and cajoling the masses while thin beggars sat on the outskirts, pleading for scraps. Scattered throughout the crowd, Phrable Centurions kept the peace, easily identified by their silver helmets adorned with tall yellow plumes.

After several minutes of moving through the crowd, Eon called a halt. Jek and Ven immediately pulled poles from the wagon to set up the stall. Anto looked around, confused. Although there were people and stalls everywhere, this was not the noisy, turbulent marketplace he was expecting. There was no yelling, no hawking. People moved from stall to stall, looking and buying in a quiet, calm manner. Shaking his head in bewilderment, he focused on helping the others set up. Mar brought out a small round table and placed a cloth over the top, then another smaller cloth on that. She stood at the table, smiling out at the crowd. Even before they had finished displaying their fruits and vegetables, someone approached. After looking over the produce, the woman slipped her hands under the top cloth on the table. Silently, the woman and Mar moved their fingers under the cloth. After a moment, the woman nodded and smiled. She removed her hands and reached for her purse. Mar spoke to Jek and he gathered the woman's order. Mar and the woman exchanged fruit for money, and the transaction was complete.

"What...what just happened?" Anto whispered to Ven from the side.

"What do you mean?"

"They never said anything to each other. They just wiggled their fingers under that cloth."

Ven laughed lightly. "That's how we conduct business. By moving their fingers in certain patterns, touching in set ways, they negotiate the price. Haven't you ever been to a market before?"

Anto shook his head. "This is so different from what I've seen."

"What do you mean?"

"The markets I've been to are noisy, with everyone yelling at each other and bickering over prices."

Ven shrugged. "Sounds horrible. But to each their own, I guess. Come. We still have to get the rest of the wagon emptied.

The next several hours sped by. Although still weak, Anto worked as hard as he could helping the family. Nobody commented when he had to stop and rest, his face flush and his skin clammy from exertion. Instead, they simply took over whatever chore he had been working on. The family worked well together. Mar negotiated, Ven and Anto ran to fulfill orders and Eon and Jek did small repairs for customers between the stall and the wagon. It wasn't until mid-afternoon before the crowds had thinned enough for them to relax a bit.

"What do you think, Da?" Jek asked as they gathered to share some cool water from the wooden barrel pulled from the wagon.

Eon squinted up at the sky, gauging how much daylight they had left.

"Probably get another few customers before sundown," he replied.

"Think it worth staying the night?" Mar asked.

Eon thought for a moment before answering, studying the crowd.

"Could be. Better to stay this side of the walls for the night, at the least. We can head out at first light."

"Can we explore some?" Ven asked.

Mar nodded. "Keep close, though. And be back by dusk to help pack up."

With a quick nod, Ven grabbed Anto's arm and pulled him away into the crowd.

They weaved through the people. They looked at the wares and sampled the samples. Anto kept shaking his head, not believing he was here or that he had stumbled upon such a wonderful family. They were good people. Honest people. He had instantly felt at home with them. The thought of going back, of working on a farm, with such good-hearted people was beyond any expectations he had had when he walked away from his Father. His mouth kept turning up into a smile all on its own. He hadn't known it could do that. Deep in his heart, a small fire of hope ignited. He watched as Ven tried on a hat, the smile returning again. His exhaustion was ignored. He was having more fun exploring the market with Ven than he had ever had before. Even the soreness in his muscles felt good because it was from honest, hard work. His soul let out the breath it had been holding for years and he allowed himself to relax and enjoy the afternoon. For the next couple hours, they laughed and joked, and the time went by far too quickly.

"Is that man all right?" Anto pointed to their left as they walked. Slumped against a wall was a lone person. His clothes were little more than rags, tattered and filthy. They had once been white, but now were soiled beyond cleaning. His head was completely covered by a dirty white cloth. He wasn't moving, just sitting there, head hung low between his knees.

"Stay away," Ven warned. Anto stopped, surprised by the unfamiliar tone in Ven's voice.

"What's wrong?"

"Just keep a distance from anyone wearing a cloak like that."

"Why?"

"They are the Faceless."

"Wait. What?"

"The Faceless." Ven's face was stony, his mouth tight. "They are dangerous."

"But--But that's just a story." Anto was stunned. "The Face Stealer is just a tale told to children. My mother told it to me when I was younger."

But Ven shook his head. "Not just a story. They're real. And they're dangerous."

"So he's...."

"He went to the mountain for knowledge. They took his face. Now, he waits for death to claim him. But it never will."

Anto shuddered, daring another glance at the hooded figure. Memories of long nights huddled under his blanket in terror flooded his thoughts and he shivered in the sun.

"We should get back," Ven said. "It'll be dark soon."

Anto numbly nodded, then shook himself out of his reverie. "I'm going to grab one more of those dough nuggets from that lady. Want one?"

"Sure."

Anto stepped past a knot of people, by now an expert at ducking in and out of the groups of people. He felt a commotion among the crowd and suddenly, a column of Centurions marched through the center of the throng. Anto watched as they briskly stomped by, their polished armor glinting and their yellow plumes waving. The Centurions passed. The crowd collapsed. Anto was pushed to the right. Then jostled to the left. There was a moment of chaos as people filled in the space once more. A wall of shadow rose in front of him as someone stepped up to him. He looked up but suddenly, his world went black.

He woke with a jostle. Solid iron bars were the first thing he saw. He scrambled to his feet, knocking his head on bars above him. He fell with a yelp. Every part of his body that had not already been hurting was now, especially his head. He gingerly touched his hair, feeling a sticky mess where he had been hit.

"Quiet!" a voice hissed in the murky light.

Anto looked over. A small girl cowered in a cage next to his. Her eyes were wide, and her thin arms shook as they held her knees.

"Quiet!" she whispered again. "He doesn't like it when we make noise."

"Who?"

But the girl didn't answer. She lowered her head further behind her knees. Anto looked around, steadying himself as he was jostled about. They were in the back of a wagon, that much was obvious. Four cages total, although the other two were empty. A thick tarp covered the tops of the cages, keeping out the light from outside, keeping them in gloom.

"What's going on?" Anto asked the girl. "Where are we?"

But the girl wouldn't answer, her fear too great to overcome.

Frustrated, Anto tried the bars. He studied the lock. He felt for weaknesses. Nothing. The cage was solid. He wasn't going anywhere.

"What's your name?"

But the girl simply stared at him with haunted eyes.

"We're going to get out of this," he told her. He told himself. "We are. We just need to not give up."

A jolt of the wagon sent him into the side of the cage.

"Ow!"

He got to his knees, placing a hand on the bars above his head to stop him from bashing it. Anto leaned forward, looking for something they could use to escape.

"We're going to escape," he repeated. The girl simply watched him, arms hugging her knees, eyes hooded and unblinking.

"I'm Anto."

Silence.

Huffing in frustration, he sat back. As he did, the wagon hit another bump and Anto was thrown backwards. His cage lifted when he hit. The combination of him falling and the wagon bouncing was enough to lift the far side of the cage. A split second later, it slammed back down. He looked behind him. The gate of the wagon was little more than a board of wood across the width of the bed. But that was enough to give Anto an idea.

"I'm going to try to knock my cage off the wagon," he told her. "Maybe you can too. Just throw yourself at the side when there's a bump."

Putting his words into action, Anto squatted and waited. When the wagon lurched, he threw himself at the bars. But his timing was off, and he succeeded only in bruising his arm. Undaunted, he positioned himself again. And again. And again.

Over and over, he launched himself at the side of the cage, trying to shift it every time the wagon bounced. He tried different starting positions, but nothing worked. The cage would tip up slightly, but never enough to fall over and out of the wagon. Finally, battered and bruised, he sat down and leaned against the bars, wincing at the pain. He let out a deep sigh, trying not to succumb to the despair that threatened to overwhelm him.

"I have to get back," he muttered to himself. "I have to get back to Ven and his family." He felt dry tears forming at the corners of his eyes. Dehydrated and exhausted, his body had nothing left to contribute to his sadness, but he felt the tears nevertheless. "I have to."

"Don't give up," the girl whispered in the darkness.

At first, he didn't know if he had actually heard her or if he had just heard his own thoughts. But gradually, he realized she had spoken.

"I'm trying, but I don't know if I can go on," he replied, not rising his head.

"You have to."

"What about you?"

"I'll find a way."

"How?"

"Only the Faceless know."

They sat together, alone in the dark. Anto couldn't see her anymore; the light beyond the canvas had faded to shadows. It was night yet the wagon continued to bounce along. He couldn't guess how far from Phrable they were. Was Ven looking for him? Or had they given up on someone who was essentially a stranger and left? Had he lost his chance at a happy life or was there still time?

Time passed. At some point, the wagon rattled to a stop. Anto heard footsteps outside, then the canvas was thrown back. Anto looked up. A large man, his face buried in a dense beard of wiry black, tossed a hunk of moldy bread into the cage. He did the same for the girl.

"Eat up," he snarled. "Can't have you dying before I get paid."

"Why are you doing this?" Anto choked.

The man whirled and struck the cage with a large cudgel.

"Quiet!" And he stormed off. A few minutes later, he returned, put a small cup of water on the top of each cage, then left.

Anto looked over. The girl scrambled to her haunches. She reached up and tilted the cup so the water splashed into her open mouth. She glanced over to him.

"Drink quick. Else he'll take it away."

Nodding, Anto repeated her movements. The water was brackish and slimy, but it was water. A moment later, the man returned, retrieved the cups and threw the canvas back over the cages. It wasn't long before they were bouncing along once more.

"He's a slaver," the girl said between jostles.

"What?"

"A slaver. Gets paid to take us off the streets. Sells us."

"I'm no slave."

She shrugged in the darkness, knowing his opinion was worth a lot less than his body.

"What's your name?" Anto asked again.

"Doesn't matter," came the reply. "Ask me again in the next life." And then she was silent once more.

More hours spent trying to escape. Hitting the bars. Prying at the edges with broken fingernails. Sobbing in the dark. The wagon hit a large hole and once more, the edge of the cage opposite from him lifted ever so slightly.

Another jolt. Like the universe was mocking him. Showing him escape was possible but just out of reach. His despair hardened, gave way to anger. He was going to escape. The fire was small but hot. After all he had endured, to be reduced to bondage like this was too much.

Anto moved to the front of the cage and got to his feet, crouching, staring at the back of the cage. He listened, focusing only on the sound of the wheels. Then, when he heard them fall into a rut, he launched himself. This time, his timing was perfect. The cage tilted up. He grabbed hold of the top of the cage and hung on, pushing all his weight into the bars. The cage lifted further, teetering. Anto smashed his body into the iron bars. Then, slowly, the cage shifted past the apex and suddenly, he was falling.

The cage hit the wooden board, smashing it. The cage tumbled off the wagon. Anto was thrown about, striking the metal again and again. The cage hit the road hard, knocking the wind out of Anto. He could barely breathe from the dust and trauma. His head spun and he blinked. He smelled dirt. Lifting his head, he winced from pain. A hand came away from his head bloody and dirty. Somewhere, he was aware of the wagon, no more than thirty yards away, coming to a halt. The jingle of the horse's harness snapped his attention into place.

Blinking past the dust, he pushed at the cage. He heard the wagon creak as it stopped. The bars wouldn't budge. Then one did. The fall had broken a couple. He pushed. He laid on his back and struck them with his feet. He pushed his back into them. There was a holler from the wagon, gruff and dangerous. He felt the bars dig into his side and back. Still he pushed. The bars bent, weakened by the impact.

Hearing someone in the distance, Anto squeezed through the bars, tearing his clothes and skin. He fell to the ground, free from the cage but not out of danger. The man yelled and Anto saw a shadow approaching. Getting to his feet, holding his side, he bled into the surrounding forest.

The bush was thick, but he was able to scramble through. Behind him, he heard a crashing as the slaver blundered in after him. But the large man couldn't navigate the labyrinth of branches as easily and Anto put some distance between them. Finding a cramped hollow in a rotting log, Anto squeezed in and held his breath. He heard the slaver cursing and bulling closer. But the dense bush slowed him down and, after several minutes, he let out a string of curses while backing out.

Anto tried to breathe slowly but his lungs felt like they had never tasted fresh air. Hand over mouth, he gulped air, trying to calm himself. He felt his side. The wound was shallow and, although bloody, not as bad as he had thought. He barely felt the pain anyway. It was simply another attack on his body and mind. As the weight of his situation settled, his body spasmed with dry sobs.

Ven! He had to get back to Ven. Back to the closest thing he had to a friend. He needed to believe that Ven's family was still in Phrable. Maybe even looking for him. If only he could get back in time. Before they left for their home. Did any of them say where they were from? No. He didn't remember them saying. So he had to get back. They were going to leave at first light. Unless he had already been gone for over a day. He shook his head. Didn't matter. He had to try.

Listening for the slaver, he pulled himself out of his hiding spot. He got three steps before stopping.

The girl.

The girl was still in her cage. Still locked up, waiting to be sold into a lifetime of servitude.

Anto looked back towards Phrable. Then up the road towards where the slaver had stomped off. He had nothing. No family, no friends, no food, no shelter. Not even a weapon. He had nothing. He couldn't help her. He could barely help himself, wounded and starving as he was. There was nothing he could do for her.

Five minutes later, he was running up the road, desperately trying to catch up with the slaver's wagon and stay ahead of the dreadfoxes who had already picked up the scent of fresh blood and were howling all around him in the dark.

He came upon the slaver's camp a few hours later. He had pulled the wagon off the road into a small, open area among the trees. The horses had been unhitched from the wagon. The campfire was low. Anto looked around, finally spotting the slaver asleep under the wagon. He crouched, looking around the area, not believing he would leave himself unprotected. He got on his stomach, squinting intently.

There!

A thin string stretched from tree to tree around the perimeter. He carefully followed the string. Small bells were attached near the trunks. Anyone blundering into the camp would set off the bells. And being under the wagon, the slaver would have plenty of cover to react. Anto moved carefully and slowly, working his way around the camp, looking for anything that might help. The cries of the dreadfoxes were closer. They had picked up the scent of his wound and were closing in. He needed to hurry.

He studied the sleeping hulk. He must have the keys to the cage on him somewhere. But how to get them? Anto blew out a soft breath in frustration. Maybe he could force the lock somehow. But he immediately discarded that idea. It would make too much noise. No. He needed to incapacitate the slaver first.

Another dreadfox cry, closer still. One of the horses snorted, uneasy from the sound. They would be on him in moments. Moving as quickly as he dared, Anto made his way to the horses. They snuffed but he kept as far away as possible. Stepping carefully, he found the end of one of the harness leads. Carefully, slowly, he crawled under the wagon. The slaver snored deeply, so far undisturbed. Anto took the lead and eased it under one of the slaver's feet. Careful not to pull or yank, he tied it off around the ankle of the brute. The slaver murmured and shifted, bringing his foot away. But there was plenty of length to the rope. Anto slowly wormed his way back out from under the wagon. Then, he slipped off his bloody shirt and tied it to the lead. The horses snuffed again. The scent of blood made them nervous.

Bare-chested but too scared to feel the cold night, Anto stepped up onto one of the wagon wheels. He dared not step onto the wagon itself, fearing the squeaking would waken the slaver. He prayed he was out of sight on the wheel.

Moments later, he heard movement in the surrounding brush. The horses, fully awake now and alert to the danger around them, whinnied from stress. Anto heard the slaver move just a few feet from him.

"Quiet!" he grumbled.

Then, Anto spotted a dark shadow slinking into the open. The dreadfox was more than a meter long and half as tall. Its thin nose rose into the air as it pinpointed the blood scent. Behind it, two more emerged from the bush. The horses stamped their feet and pulled on their reins. Anto had a moment of panic when he realized he hadn't checked to make sure the reins were free. If they were tied tight, the horses would not be able to run. But the slaver, like many, had only loosely thrown the reins over some branches, sure that the horses would not attempt to wander too far.

The dreadfoxes, smelling the bloody shirt next to the horses, moved quickly towards their prey. The horses cried out and pulled their reins free. The slaver, woken now by the commotion, grabbed his cudgel. The dreadfoxes leapt. The horses bolted. The slaver was pulled from under the wagon. Off into the night went the parade--horse, dreadfox and slaver-- trailing curses and dust.

Anto grabbed a large rock and climbed into the wagon, throwing the tarpaulin off the cages. Inside, the girl huddled in a corner, wide-eyed at Anto's sudden appearance.

"It's all right," he said. "I'm going to get you out!"

He smashed the rock on the lock. Flakes of rust floated to the ground and the girl covered her head at the sound. Again and again, he struck the lock until it finally gave. Anto opened the door and extended a hand.

"Let's go."

But the girl didn't move. She peaked out from behind her hands, terrified into immobility.

"He'll be back soon," Anto pleaded. "Please, we need to leave."

Her only movement was trembling.

Anto blew out a breath in frustration. She was petrified. If he reached in to grab her, who knows how she would react. But the slaver would be back soon. They were running out of time.

"Please," he tried again. "I'm not going to hurt you. We can escape. But we have to go. Now."

But there are those times when the fear is simply too great. Too big to overcome. Anto reached in. She pushed herself against the bars, keeping as far away as possible.

"All right," he relented, removing his hand and standing back. "I'm going to leave. But you need to as well. He'll be back soon."

Reluctantly, Anto stepped off the wagon. He hesitated, looking back, but when there was no movement, he sighed and turned away. He rummaged around the slaver's belonging, grabbing a dirty shirt to cover himself. He hurried away, taking an angle so she could watch him leave the area. He moved into the surrounding bush but didn't go far. Instead, he stopped among the covering branches, and watched, waiting for her to exit her prison.

He settled in. In the distance, he saw the sky begin to lighten. Dawn was approaching. As he crouched among the leaves, the adrenaline wore off and weariness seeped into his muscles. His body ached from the fall. He touched the wound in his side. The bleeding had finally stopped, leaving a crusty mess. His eyelids were heavy, but he refused to let them drop. Not here, not until the girl got safely away. But an hour later, she still hadn't come out. A brilliant red sky signaled the start of a long, hot day.

Then, in the distance, he heard something. Daring to look, he saw a figure moving towards the camp, lurching along the road. Even though the shape was far away, Anto immediately knew it was the slaver. His curses floated ahead of him down the road. Anto looked to the wagon. Still no sign of the girl.

Move! He hurtled the thought at the wagon. *Get out of there!* He forced his body to remain still. The slaver was steadily approaching. Anto looked around for a weapon. Perhaps he could knock the brute out and give the girl more time. He looked down at his hands, shaking from exhaustion and hunger and wondered if he could get at least one blow in before the slaver beat him to death.

But then, movement caught his eye. He turned to see the girl slip away, quiet as a mouse. She disappeared into the brush on the far side of the wagon. Anto breathed a heavy sigh of relief. She was safe. He set off in the opposite direction, away from the camp and the road, leaving before the slaver heard him moving through the bush.

He walked until he couldn't move anymore. Then, he found a hollow amid a dense bank of bramble and passed out. When he woke, the sun had already passed overhead and was beginning its descent. He had slept most of the day. Anto crawled from his spot, wincing at the stiffness and soreness. He rummaged some dragonberries and found water in a thin creek. Then he crawled back into the hollow and fell asleep, shivering in the cold of night but alive, if only barely.

When he next woke, the first thought that penetrated the fog of sleep was fuzziness. Not fuzziness of thought, but fuzziness of fur. He opened his eyes and looked towards his stomach. Curled up next to him, sharing body heat, was a small animal. It was covered in fine tawny brown and red fur. As Anto watched, it uncurled to stretch. A long snout opened, and the creature yawned. Anto noticed rows of needle-teeth and a long pink tongue. Its eyes were all black. Its ears were small and triangular. Its paws were almost human-like, with four jointed fingers. Its tail, as long as its body, flapped back and forth lazily. After its yawn, it looked Anto in the eyes. They studied each other for a moment. Then the creature turned its head, gave Anto's hand a lick, and closed its eyes, snuggling up against his chest for some more sleep.

Anto smiled and gently placed an arm around the animal. He recognized it as a quipen. Quipens were smart and quick, a cross in looks, agility and attitude between a fox, a cat and a racoon. And they usually ended up as meals for the larger, faster dreadfoxes. Apparently this one had decided to use Anto as shelter. The small animal's body next to him gave him a purpose, however small. At least for the moment, something needed him. Death wouldn't be so bad if he was able to keep that little creature safe for a few moments, he decided before closing his eyes.

When he woke next, the quipen was gone. Anto lifted himself to his elbow, scanning the hollow in a panic. His body felt like it was encased in stone it was so stiff. He winced as he moved, forcing his muscles to bend and flex. From his right, a chirp greeted him. There was the quipen, a small pile of dragonberries at its feet. It was sitting upright, like a human, and grasping a bit of fruit between its hands, its long snout dyed orange with the juice of a dragonberry.

"Hi there, little one," Anto smiled. The quipen tilted its head, watching him with no fear, only curiosity. "Are any of those berries for me?"

The quipen tilted its head the other way, reached down and rolled two berries from the pile in his direction.

Anto laughed. "Only two? I guess I better look for my own breakfast then."

The quipen nodded its head once, then gathered its breakfast and scampered outside. Anto slowly followed, his body unwilling to move. It was morning again. The air was fresh and the few clouds in the sky weren't looking like they would trouble the sun. Anto picked some berries and drank from the stream. The quipen followed him, keeping easy pace on its four long legs. It moved almost like a cat, but with distinctive human characteristics. It was intelligent, that much was obvious. Anto watched as it slinked along the shore of the creek, sniffing and digging, finding grubs and worms. It would then sit up on its haunches and eat, holding the snack in both hands. It would regularly look at Anto, squeaking or purring or chirping.

"I need to go," he told the quipen. "I can't stay here, as nice as it is. I must find a town. Maybe I can still find Ven. Or the girl."

The quipen looked sideways at him and continued munching on a grub.

Anto sighed. "But I don't know which direction to go."

He looked around. Forest surrounded him on all sides. In one direction he knew was the road. But also, the slaver. Or others like him. Where was safety? Where could he go? Once more, he strained his thoughts, trying to remember if Ven or his family had mentioned where they were from. But he only knew they went to the silent market at Phrable once in a while. So, if he wanted to reunite with them, he'd need to find his way back there.

He thought he remembered which way lay the road. He kept that direction to his left and began walking, hoping to go parallel to the road and eventually reach the city. His progress was slow. He was weak, hungry and either too hot or too cold. But every time he slumped down on to a log, the quipen was there, nudging him for a scratch or purring around his feet. Then it would scamper into the bush and return a few moments later with more dragonberries. It offered Anto grubs and bugs but Anto politely declined, not quite desperate enough to eat them, although his stomach grumbled. Thankfully, there were plenty of berries and other edible plants in the area and, although he was never full, nor was he starving.

Two days passed. He trudged ever forward, encouraged by the strange animal that had adopted him. During the hot days, the quipen found all the trickles of fresh water and shady stones to rest. During the cool nights, they wrapped themselves around each other, sharing body heat and safety.

Eventually, the trees fell off and he found himself in a wide field of grass. Seeing a small hill, he trudged over. From its top, he could see a little better. The road the slaver travelled was behind him, little more than a break in the surrounding forest, far in the distance. He had unknowingly wandered further and further from it over the past several days. In front of him was a vast countryside of rolling hills, scattered groups of trees and thin streams. But far in the distance, he thought he could see buildings. Figuring that was as good a direction as any, he walked. As he moved, his muscles warmed, bringing fresh pains and aches. Everything was sore, either from injury or malnutrition. But there was a small spark within him still, forcing him to put one foot in front of the other and not give up.

The quipen followed him, seemingly unconcerned with directions or goals. Looking down at the scampering creature, Anto couldn't help but smile.

"I see a town in the distance. I think I'm going to go there. Would you like to come with me?"

The quipen chirped a response, rubbing against his leg.

"All right then." He looked out over the countryside again, squinting to see better. As he descended the hill, the faraway town disappeared behind trees, leaving them alone in the wilderness.

The quipen chirped from beside his foot. Anto stopped.

"What is it?"

A moment later, it had scrambled up his leg and torso and was sitting contently on top of his head, its long tail wrapped around the back of his neck. Anto was surprised at how light it was. It felt like he was wearing a particularly fuzzy hat, nothing more. The quipen chirped and patted Anto's forehead.

"I guess you need a rest, huh? Well? What do you think? Towards the town on the horizon?"

The quipen squeaked, rubbed its nose and scratched its ear.

"I'll take that as a yes."

The day passed quietly, a welcome relief from the stress and uncertainty of the last few days. When not riding on his head, the quipen scampered through the tall grass, occasionally poking its head above the blades or leaping after some small prey. It squeaked and twittered happily, never more than a few meters from Anto as he walked across the fields. Every once in a while, the quipen would run back to Anto, scurry up his body and rest atop his head, blissfully unconcerned with anything but a nap.

By the time the sun was setting, they were more than halfway to the town. They found a quiet, sheltered spot among some large boulders and settled in. As dusk deepened, the air turned cool but, with no means of making a fire, they had to content themselves with each other's body heat. The quipen curled up next to Anto, snuggling close to his chest, wrapping it long tail around its body.

"You know," Anto whispered in the dark, "if you're going to stay with me, you'll need a name."

The quipen yawned and gave his hand a lick.

"Erishgal? Kesin? No. Maybe Anatu?"

Suddenly, it raised its head. A low growl rumbled in its small chest.

Click. Click. Whistle.

"What it is?"

It sprang to its feet, dashing past Anto's head. Anto rolled over, getting to his hands and knees. The quipen leapt to the top of one of the boulders and let out a shrill bark. Anto jumped up next to it. Below them, just on the other side of the boulder, was a dreadfox.

It was frozen, caught in the act of sneaking up on them. The quipen barked again. Now, the dreadfox gathered its hindquarters, preparing to leap. Anto looked around for anything to use as a weapon. Finding a small rock, he threw it at the dreadfox. The beast easily slid out of the way. A long tongue licked the side of its muzzle, anticipating a quipen dinner.

But Anto's companion had other ideas. Instead of running away, the quipen's fur stood up and it barked again. The dreadfox, ten times as large, snuffed and pawed the ground, readying itself to dash in, grab its prey, and escape. Then, just as Anto readied another rock, the quipen leapt off the boulder straight at the dreadfox. The dreadfox, surprised by the move, backed up a pace. The quipen landed in front of the dreadfox and swiped at it with its paw, scratching its nose. The dreadfox yelped and leapt back. The quipen barked and swiped again. Not knowing how to handle such tiny fierceness, the dreadfox slowly backed up. Growling, it snapped. The quipen was a flash of fur as it leapt out of the way. Anto hit its flank with a rock. The quipen barked and swiped again. The dreadfox was still not ready to give up its meal so easily, but a well-aimed rock from Anto to its shoulder finally convinced it that the prey wasn't worth the trouble and it turned, loping off into the night.

After a moment of listening, the quipen jumped back up to Anto's side. Anto sat down on the rock, gently checking the quipen for injuries and scratching behind its ears.

"Well, I think I know what your name is," he said with a laugh. "Only someone as brave as Telos himself would take on such a monstrous foe and win."

The quipen purred as Anto continued to scratch under its chin.

"What do you think? Do you mind if I call you Telos?"

In response, Telos licked his finger and purred louder.

They reached the village late the next morning. It was little more than a sleepy hamlet perched along a lazy river. Telos sat upright on top of Anto's head, curious at all the sights and smells. They, in turn, got more than a few curious glances as they entered the town.

"Excuse me," Anto stopped a man, his arms full of boxes of metal bits bound, no doubt, for the smithy.

"Yes?"

"Can you tell me how far this place is from Phrable?"

"Not more than a day's ride," he replied.

"Really? That's great!"

The man grunted and continued on his way. Anto hurried to catch up with him.

"I don't suppose you know anyone who would be willing to give me a ride, do you?"

"Mum Gwinth goes that way once a week. Mayhap you can earn a ride with some work."

Anto's heart lifted a little. Maybe, just maybe, he could still find someone in Phrable who knew where Ven and his family came from.

"Mum Gwinth. Thank you. Er, and where--?"

The man sighed, shifting the boxes in his arms. "Next street over. All the way to the end. You'll see a sign." And with that, he picked up his pace, leaving Anto and Telos alone.

Five minutes later, they had toured the entire town. It was little more than a collection of well-worn houses built with wood from the surrounding forest. In some ways, it reminded Anto of his home, but warmer and friendlier. Everyone he passed offered up a smile or quick greeting. Even Telos purred contently from atop his head. Soon, they were standing in front of a small shop. A faded wooden sign hung over the door, proclaiming the store as 'Gwinth's Goodes'.

"I guess this is the place."

Telos chirped in agreement.

"Now, don't steal anything, Telos. We need her to get us to Phrable."

Telos batted his ear to show his displeasure.

The first thing they noticed when they stepped inside were the smells. Cinnamon and sugar. Freshly cut flowers and finely sifted flour. Anto's stomach rumbled, desperate for something other than dragonberries. He eyed the stacks of fresh bread and loaves of cheese. Telos let out a squeak from atop his head.

"I know. I'm hungry too. But business first," he said firmly.

"Hullo, hullo!"

Coming out from the back of the store was a small woman, no higher than Anto's shoulders. Her well-lined face was open and bright and there was a twinkle to her eyes that lit up the little shop. She dusted her hands off on the apron wrapped snugly around her round stomach and eyed them.

"Looking for something to eat, are ya?"

"Yes, I mean, not really."

She gave him a well-natured frown. "By the looks of it, you haven't had a decent meal in some time."

"That's, um, that's why we're here. I'm trying to get back to my, er, family. In Phrable. I was told you go there."

"Aye. Once a week for supplies. And occasionally a nip of brandy." She giggled into her hand.

"Well, I was hoping to ride with you next time. I'll work for passage, of course."

She eyed him critically from head to toe and back up again, seeing little more than a malnourished scrawny boy. Telos chirped from his head and she smiled.

"Not many bond with a quipen. Very rare. Where did you find him?"

"He found me, to be honest."

Mum Gwinth nodded. "Hmm."

"I call him Telos."

"Hoo hoo. Grand name, that is. Powerful name."

"He's lives up to the name," he assured her. Telos leaned forward, sniffing at her. He climbed down to Anto's shoulder. Anto held out his arm for Telos to walk along, until he was able to reach out and touch Mum Gwinth's hand. She smiled warmly, letting him get used to her. Then, without warning, Telos jumped the gap and scrambled up onto her shoulder, wrapping around her neck and purring.

"Oh hoo!" She chortled. "I passed your test then, yes?"

Telos licked her ear, eliciting another giggle from her.

"Well," she said, reaching up and petting Telos, "I think we can work something out, young master."

The next several days passed quickly and enjoyably. Anto helped Mum Gwinth--for that was how she was always referred to, not Gwinth, not Mum, but Mum Gwinth--with various chores around the shop. She was more than happy to have an extra pair of strong hands. Although she had no room in her small private quarters above the store, she insisted Anto and Telos sleep in the small storage room in the back of the shop. Telos, for his part, quickly became the unofficial mascot of 'Gwinth's Goodes'. The townspeople delighted in his antics and he turned away not a single pet or scratch. And if he occasionally stole a stray fruit? Well, Mum Gwinth always seemed to be looking the other way whenever that happened.

Mum Gwinth made sure they were fed well every evening. Sturdy stews, fresh breads, hand-picked vegetables. Anto could literally feel his body rebuilding itself after so many hardships. The food, together with the active work, helped him recover quickly and the week passed too swiftly.

"Time to pack." The words, though he knew were coming, were bittersweet. As wonderful as his time with Mum Gwinth had been, Anto was anxious to track down Ven and his family. He lifted various crates and boxes into the wagon, mostly produce that was not selling or other odd trinkets she hoped would garner interest in a bigger market like Phrable. As he loaded the wagon, Mum Gwinth hitched the horses and locked the shop.

By mid-morn they were on the road. It was an easy ride with easy talk. Mum Gwinth had an instinctual sense of when to speak and when to let others do the talking. She never asked about his past yet, through her kindness and patience, learned most of it. Sometimes, she simply allowed the wind and birds and the creaking of the wagon be their companions.

Phrable was as busy and bewildering as he remembered. Wide avenues full of wagons and carriages, narrow alleys full of shadows and danger. People everywhere. And then the Silent Market, the quiet center of the storm. As Anto helped Mum Gwinth set up a small table and stand, he scanned the crowd, searching for a familiar face. They didn't have much to sell and were finished quickly.

"Go," Mum Gwinth said to him. "Go find your family."

"Are you sure?" he asked, eager yet unwilling to simply abandon someone who had shown him so much kindness.

In response, she patted his arm. "I've been doing this by myself for many a season, young master. Go. I look forward to meeting them."

Anto smiled and nodded his thanks. Telos scrambled up onto Anto's head and they let the crowd take them away.

By late afternoon, Anto was sweaty, Telos was irritable, and they had not found Ven or his family. Weary and despondent, they returned to Mum Gwinth. She was laughing and talking with two other matrons, a small bottle freely passing between them. From the looks of it, she had not sold a single item but, judging by the look on her face, that had never really been the point of the trip. Despite his mood, Anto had to smile at the simple happiness of her life.

Indeed, she welcomed him back with a broad laugh. Seeing he no one walking with him, she immediately understood the situation and quickly brought together some food and drink for them. The women gossiped for a few minutes while Anto and Telos wolfed down the food, then excused themselves.

"What a day, what a day," she said after they had spent several minutes watching the throng in silence. "All these people but barely any sales."

Anto grunted, struggling to find some kind words amid his dark storm of thoughts. Mum Gwinth saw that storm and headed it off.

"I don't suppose you'd be willing to help me load it all back up into the cart?"

"Of course, I will help," he replied automatically, grateful for the distraction.

She nodded. From there, they worked quietly but efficiently. Before long, the wagon had been repacked, minus some fruit and vegetables for the beggars in the market. Mum Gwinth hauled herself up onto the seat and simply but firmly patted the spot next to her. Without a word, Anto and Telos joined her, and they began the journey back to Creekslope.

And so started a summer more enjoyable than he had thought possible. He had despaired when he found no sign of Ven, wondering what he was going to do. But Mum Gwinth brought him and Telos into her world seamlessly and without question, giving his life a purpose. Work around the shop was hard but rewarding. The people of Creekslope were unassuming, kind and honest. Once a week, they loaded the wagon and spent the day in Phrable—Anto searching for Ven and Mum Gwinth gossiping with her friends. But as the days grew shorter, he looked less and less. Ven gradually faded in his mind. That it took him most of the summer to realize he had a new family with Telos and Mum Gwinth was a source of shame for him. Shame that he fought down by working that much harder for her, doing extra work, shouldering more of the responsibilities of the store.

Telos, free to roam as he pleased, spent the days either hunting in the surrounding fields or soaking up the attention of the townspeople. He learned every open window that promised food, every nook and cranny that yielded a tasty grub and every hand that never denied him a satisfying scratch behind the ears.

Their lives were busy and hard, but full of goodness and honesty. More than once during the summer, Anto caught himself smiling for no reason. Up until those days, he had never known how full his life and his heart could be. The days piled up and too soon, the crops were ready for harvesting and the nights were turning cool.

"Rain's coming soon," Mum Gwinth said to him one day late in the summer as they were loading up the wagon.

"Yeah?"

She nodded. "Can smell it on the wind."

Anto looked up at the beautiful blue expanse above him. Nothing more than a puffy ball of white could be seen. But by then, he knew better than to question her.

"We'll get in one, maybe two more trips," she continued, "then we'll have to wait out the rains. Roads become a muddy mess."

"How long?"

She shrugged. "Can usually start up again after the flox bloom."

That would be several moons. Anto nodded, realizing his chances of reuniting with Ven were slim and getting slimmer. But it didn't bother him as much as he thought it would. There was a longing to see his friend, to be sure. Yet life was moving on.

"What will we do until then?"

She laughed. "Well, I would usually be busy readying the shop for the rains and cold. But you're a bit more suited for chopping wood and nailing shingles than these old bones, I think."

"You're not old," he protested.

"Old enough to know you'd be about it quicker. Besides, you're still too skinny. Need to get some heft to your weight."

Anto laughed. While it was true that he was healthy once more, he still hadn't regained the weight lost during his wandering in the wild.

"I'll do my best. But something tells me you can swing an axe better than I."

"Well, of that, there's no doubt. But you won't get better if you don't practice."

Anto laughed again and Mum Gwinth snapped the reins, beginning one of their last trips to Phrable for the season.

"Mum Gwinth, can you teach me how to negotiate with my fingers like you do?" he asked on the journey home.

She gave him a glance out of the side of her eye.

"It takes many years of practice to learn the subtleties," she responded. "If you don't know the art well, you will be easy pickings."

"We have all rainy season," he grinned.

Mum Gwinth smiled. Perhaps the off season wouldn't be so bad after all.

When Anto was nineteen years old:

Three years slipped past.

Anto grew into his body, becoming a well-proportioned young man. Mum Gwinth looked at him with the pride of an adoptive mother. And, truth be told, Anto came to think of her as family as well. She was nurturing but firm, kind but stern. Life took on an easy rhythm. The stress and hurt of his past slid off him without his even realizing it. Long-ago trauma was still there, of course, but was scabbed over with everyday responsibilities. Mum Gwinth and Telos depended on him. He depended on them. There were more immediate concerns: canning vegetables, shoeing the horses, sweeping and stocking the store. These were the thoughts that occupied Anto's mind.

Trips to Phrable for gossip and selling. Long days of customers and stocking, weeding and mending. Routines that, normal enough and boring for so many, were a welcome balm on Anto's soul. As the seasons rolled by, Mum Gwinth would occasionally skip a Phrable trip, sometimes saying she was too tired for the trip or that her trick knee was acting up again. Those trips, Anto would practice his skill at silently negotiating under the cloth with patrons. He had strict orders from Mum Gwinth on prices and so forth and turned away more than a few patrons he knew were trying to take advantage of him. After a few hours of selling, Anto and Telos would then usually spend time in the late afternoon wandering the market and surrounding streets, meeting other vendors, tasting exotic foods and generally enjoying the life in the city.

During those years, the Silent Market continued to expand and grow. More and more people came from the surrounding towns and villages to trade. Phrable kept expanding to accommodate the additional populace, spilling out over the old walls. Every trip, they saw new sections being constructed. New buildings. New streets. Anto was always amazed at just how many people lived in the area. He delighted in meeting them. Learning their customs and tasting their food. A world was open to him that he had never even considered as a child. No longer was he isolated and scared. He was growing up and growing into the world around him. Creekslope was home, cozy and known, but Phrable was the adventure. A city of endless possibilities.

One afternoon, as they floated along with the crowd, going nowhere in particular, Anto heard a commotion somewhere in front of them. Telos stood up on his head and peered around. Then he bent down, blocking Anto's view.

"Hey!"

Squeak. Chitter. Chitter. Whistle.

"What's going on?"

Click. Click. Whistle.

"Danger?"

But before Telos could respond, the crowd separated. They were pushed back. There was yelling. Screaming, as if someone was scared. It sounded far away but the crowd was panicking right next to them. Anto craned his neck to see over shoulders and gasped.

Stumbling through the middle of the market was broken figure of a person. Tattered clothes hung off from a body little more than bones. Raw fingertips purple and infected. But when Anto looked to their face, his heart stopped and his breath died in his chest.

They didn't have one.

Instead, their head was a mass of skin. Shallow bowls of flesh instead of eyes. A slight ridge to suggest a lost nose. Smooth skin where ears should stick out. The jaws moved as the person screamed but there was no mouth for the noise to exit their body, only more skin keeping the scream inside.

An irrational fear grabbed Anto as he stared at the Faceless. The person was not human anymore. Cut off from humanity yet cursed to continue living, they were repulsive. Unsettling.

The person, Anto couldn't tell if they were a man or woman, lurched from place to place, unseeing and unable to ask for help. They didn't even have ears to hear the cries of terror and harsh words hurtled by the crowd.

"Get out of here!"

"Leave us be!"

"Faceless!"

Memories of old tales, told in the dark, flooded Anto's head. He remembered his Mother telling him about the Face Stealer when he was a small child. He remembered being too scared to cry out in the night, for fear of the Faceless coming for him. But even those nightmares were nothing compared to seeing one right in front of him. Stumbling. Moaning. Grasping.

Telos' whistle of warning snapped him out of his reverie just as the Faceless staggered towards them. Suddenly, a pair of strong hands grabbed hold and yanked him out of the way. The Faceless stumbled past, oblivious to him.

Anto shivered as the fear worked its way through his skin.

"Didn't I tell you to stay away from them?" a voice asked.

Anto turned. Standing there, holding him, was Ven.

"Ven? Ven??" Anto flung himself into Ven's arms, startling Telos. The hug lasted forever and an instant.

"I almost didn't recognize you," Ven laughed, finally taking a step back. "You don't look like a scarecrow anymore."

"And you've gotten taller."

Ven had indeed grown a bit. They both had. Ven was a bit shorter but had wider shoulders. His hair was cut short, framing his grinning, tanned face well. They took a minute to assess each other, smiling. Telos climbed down to Anto's shoulder and reached out, touching Ven's cheek.

"And who's this?"

"This is Telos."

"Hello, Telos. Nice to meet you." Ven gently held out his hand, palm up. Telos gave it a sniff, then rubbed his face on it, allowing the petting to commence. Ven laughed and happily obliged.

They left the middle of the crowd, finding a quiet spot next to a building along the outskirts of the market where they could talk.

"What happened to you?" Ven asked. "We looked for hours, but you had disappeared. Did I scare you off?"

"No! Gods, no. I was kidnapped."

"What?"

Anto nodded. He told Ven how the slaver had knocked him out and threw him in a cage.

"It took a couple days to escape. By then, I knew you were long gone. I was lost, starving. I ran into the woods. I barely survived."

Ven reached out and placed a hand on his shoulder. "I'm so sorry. I didn't know."

Anto took a deep breath, quelling the tears. "Telos here found me. He saved me. He really did."

Telos chirped and rubbed against Anto.

"Eventually, we found our way to a town. I've been living there ever since. I help out a shopkeeper. That's why I'm here, actually. Once a week during the dry season, we come up here to market. I looked for you, every time we came here. But--"

"We don't make it up to Phrable much," Ven admitted. "Crops haven't been that great the past few seasons. Haven't had much to sell here."

"I'm sorry to hear that."

He shrugged. "Nothing we can do about it. But you. You've had quite an adventure."

"Don't know if I'd call it that," Anto shook his head. "But what about you? How are you? How's the family, other than the crops?"

"Da passed a few seasons ago."

"What? Oh no. I'm so sorry." Now it was Anto's turn to comfort.

"It's hard, but Ma is doing all right. Jek and I help out as much as we can. They're all here today. We decided to take a chance and see if anyone needed some repairs done for some extra coin." He waved at the market around them. "Do you want to say hi?"

"Of course!"

They quickly worked their way through the crowd. What followed was a round of hugs and smiles. Even though he had only known them for a couple of days years ago, they remembered him vividly.

"You don't easily forget a half-dead boy slumped alongside the road who passed out from eating an apple," Mar laughed.

They enjoyed talking and laughing. But Anto was aware of how far the sun had slid across the sky and reluctantly looked at them.

"I need to leave soon. I still have to get the wagon back to Creekslope. It'll be dark before I get home as it is."

"Creekslope?" Ven asked.

Anto nodded. "I help Mum Gwinth at her shop there."

"That's not too far."

"No. Only a few hours. Still, I better get on the road."

"Safer if you're not alone," Mar said with a wink to Ven. "Especially as dusk settles in."

"Would," Anto turned to Ven, a spark of hope in his heart, "would you like to come with us? But I wouldn't be able to bring you back until next week. There's too much to do around the shop."

"Ma?"

Mar nodded. "Not much to do this week as far as the crops go."

"Have that fence to mend, but I can take care of it," Jek added. "Shouldn't be a problem."

"Are you sure the shopkeeper won't mind?"

Anto shrugged. "If she does, you can camp outside," he laughed.

"Deal," Ven replied with a grin.

And with that, the three of them said their farewells. Looking up, Anto guessed they would finish the last hour or so of the journey in the dark. But he already felt better knowing he wouldn't be alone. Within a few minutes, they were on the road and heading to Creekslope.

"I can't believe your Ma would let you come with me," Anto said. "We barely know each other, when you think about it."

Ven shrugged. "You're a good person. That's easy to see. Right from the beginning, she saw that you meant no harm to any of us."

"Still."

"I can jump off and still catch up with them, if that would make you feel better."

Anto turned and saw the grin on Ven's face. He gave his shoulder a punch.

"No way. After all this time, I finally get a chance to get to know you better. You're coming with me."

"Yes, sir." Another grin. Another punch.

Several minutes passed in comfortable quiet. They listened to the birds and the wheels, letting the breeze tell them the forest's gossip. After a while, Anto realized Ven was murmuring under his breath. Memories of their first meeting flooded his mind.

"You're making a songline, aren't you?"

Ven grinned and blushed. "Yeah."

"Sing to me."

"Really?"

Anto nodded. "Yeah. I'd like that."

Ven smiled and took a breath.

"The road runs straight till the hedge of heather,

Gentle to the right, over three hills,

Then follow the stream til the bridge.

Cross o'er and chase the late-day sun,

Past three crossroads without a turn."

Anto smiled. "How do you remember all that?"

Ven shrugged. "I don't know. I just like to sing. It helps pass the time."

"And you never get lost."

"Haven't yet."

They laughed. The remainder of the journey was filled with singing and laughing and smiles.

It was dark by the time they reached Creekslope, but that wasn't unusual. Often, Mum Gwinth would get caught up with her friends and they would get a late start back to the shop. Still, Anto and Ven worked quickly and quietly to unhitch and groom the horses, unload the wagon and secure everything before turning in for night.

Years ago, once it was settled that Anto and Telos would stay with Mum Gwinth, Anto had built a small room attached to the back of the store for his personal space. He felt his face redden as he opened the door and showed it to Ven.

"It's not much," he started.

"You started with that corner, didn't you?" Ven asked, pointing to the near right.

"Yeah. How did you know?"

"Your joint work is much better on the other side. You learned a lot while you built this."

"I did." Reddened face, but now for a slightly different reason. "It was a learn-as-you-go project."

"Good job."

"It's all right."

They stood for a moment, looking around the small space. Telos, tired from the day, curled up at the head of the bed as usual. Ven eyed the bed.

"I can sleep on the floor."

"I only have the one blanket. So you take it."

"No."

"I insist. You're my guest."

"All right then."

They awkwardly settled in, Anto on the bed and Ven on the floor. The night was cool, and a chill settled over them within an hour. Even Ven, with the thin blanket, shivered himself awake. Silently, he moved to the bed, draping the blanket over them both. Anto, awake, shifted over, giving him as much room as he could. They both eventually fell asleep, warmed by each other's body heat.

Anto had come clean about his 'family' in Phrable long ago so Mum Gwinth was surprised and delighted to finally meet Ven. She made sure they both had a hearty breakfast of eggs, bacon and bread and then promptly put them to work.

Mum Gwinth had an innate ability to find work to do, no matter the time or place. A job that was just enough for Anto for years suddenly needed two people. For his part, Ven was more than happy to pitch in. In fact, as the week progressed, they all came up with the idea of Ven spending a week helping at the shop, then Anto helping Ven's family on their farm. And so, on the next trip to Phrable, Mum Gwinth and Mar hammered out the details of the agreement over brandy and laughter. So began a new, wonderful chapter in Anto's life.

For three moons, they were together, running the store, working the fields, helping with chores. Anto, Telos and Mum Gwinth became an extended part of Ven's family. They supported each other. They worked together and ate together. When at Ven's, Anto had his own room. The family owned a decently sized farmhouse and occasionally took on farm hands. Anto was given one of the rooms. While in Creekslope, they had to share Anto's small space but, although neither said a word about it, they both preferred it to the large, mostly empty farmhouse. Many were the nights Anto fell asleep from watching Ven's breathing, many were the mornings he woke up with Ven's arm unknowingly draped over his side.

As the days rolled past, Anto felt his heart relax a little. Even after the easy years with Mum Gwinth, he had a hard time opening up to others. Mum Gwinth asked few questions, always sensing the answers before Anto anyway. She was intuitive and wise and gave him the space and time to sort through his feelings on his own. Ven, on the other hand, would press for him to express himself and Anto struggled to do so. Many times, he had to go off looking for mushrooms by himself or spend an afternoon on the roof fixing loose planks. Anything to get away and spend time with his thoughts. During those hours, Ven would disappear, anxious yet respectful. Eventually, Anto would wrap his head around his feelings, and they would find each other, apologizing for whatever harsh words had been spoken.

Despite their constant closeness though, they rarely argued. When they did, it was easy enough to find something to take their minds off the disagreement until they were ready to work it out. There was always plenty of work to do. When they needed time apart, they had it. They learned each other's habits and dreams. How the corner of Ven's mouth turned up when he was kidding. How Anto jiggled his right leg when he was nervous. While at the farm, they often laid in an open field long into the night, watching the stars, talking about nothing, letting Telos live out his dreams of being a great hunter, patrolling the tall grass for grubs and bugs.

The market was busy. The weather was good, and spirits were high. Anto and Telos wandered through the crowd while Ven watched the stall. Anto allowed himself a smile. The sun felt good on his face. Absently, he reached up and stroked Telos' fur. Telos bent down and licked his hand in response before resuming his lookout position. A moment later, he gave a warning chirp. Anto had learned to trust the quipen so he stopped, eliciting a curse from the person walking behind them.

"What is it?"

Telos chirped again and shifted his weight.

The crowd parted and Anto saw a procession cross the area. A line of white-robed men and women, single-file and led by a priestess with a tall mitre, moved silently through the crowd.

Everyone moved out of their way, giving them wide berth. The priestess clutched no tome nor chanted no hymn. They didn't make any eye contact or interact with the crowd in any way. They simply walked, steadily and unrelentingly, through the market.

"Who are they, I wonder?" Anto said, mostly to Telos.

"The Church of the Faceless," a woman at his side replied, evidently thinking he had been speaking to her.

"Church of the Faceless?"

She nodded. "Odd ones, they are."

"You can't mean they worship the Face Stealer?"

She shrugged. "People can believe what they want." And she moved off into the crowd.

Shaking his head, Anto suppressed a shiver and turned around. He suddenly needed to be around Ven.

When the days grew shorter and clouds massed on the horizon, they knew their time together would need to be put on hold until spring. Neither Ven's family nor Mum Gwinth would risk the muddy, rutted roads to Phrable for the next few moons.

"You take care of yourself," Ven said to him as they were finishing loading their respective wagons, almost ready to go in opposite directions for the first time in moons.

"I will. You too. Keep an eye out for that bogill. It's probably still around."

Ven nodded. The creature, a sort of wild ape, was spotted lurking along the edges of their fields earlier in the season.

"Don't worry. I'm the best shot with an arrow in the area."

"Not better than me."

"So better than you!"

They grinned at each other, reluctant to end the conversation but knowing the sun was sinking and they needed to be on their way.

"Well, I guess I'll see you later." Anto managed a small smile.

Ven let out a small chuckle. "I'll probably see you first."

"You do have that habit."

They embraced, hugging each other tightly, trying to absorb as much of the other as they could before finally letting go.

When the rains came, they came with a fury. Streams surged over their banks. Roads were washed away. Fields were turned into lakes and the folk of Creekslope worried if they would have any land left to plant on come spring.

With the damp came a chill that settled into Mum Gwinth's chest. As the days sloshed past, Anto worked constantly at chasing the dampness from the store and her room. He kept the fires burning day and night, quickly depleting their store of wood. And he always kept a butter lamp going in her room to keep the darkness at bay. In between, he roamed the sodden countryside, bringing back load after load of wood to keep the flames fed. For a span during the darkest days, her chest rattled and Anto feared the worst. Not broth nor blanket, salve nor sigil helped. Telos, for his part, spent most of his time curled up next to her, giving her his heat and love. Somehow, her soul clung to her body and though considerably weakened at the end of the rains, she was still with them.

Even still, when the blue peeked through the gray overhead, Mum Gwinth was bedridden. Anto hovered over her anxiously until she shooed him out of the room.

"There's seeds to ready," she told him firmly. "Muck to clear. You have enough to do. You don't need to sit around my bed like the reaper Himself."

"I'm not hovering," he protested.

"Shoo!"

He was glad when he was finally able to throw open the windows and let fresh air clear out the staleness. Telos bounded across the drying fields, stretching his legs and happily running back and forth. Anto stood in the sun, letting its warmth touch his soul. He helped Mum Gwinth move into the sunlight as well, hoping it would finally chase the damp from inside her.

Thoughts of Phrable and Ven crossed his mind from time to time in the quieter moments. He longed to see his friend again but refused to leave Mum Gwinth alone. She was too weak. She scolded him, saying she was fine even though they both knew that wasn't true. Anto pushed down his worry, concentrating on getting her healthy again, on keeping her business running until she was ready to take over again.

At some point during that time, Anto turned twenty, a fact known to none of them.

When Anto was twenty years old:

Anto tried not to curse the sun. He was outside, shirtless and dirty, working the fields. He needed to sun's warmth to help keep Mum Gwinth comfortable as she sat by the window in her room or on the porch, but the sweat dripping off his body made it difficult to tolerate. He straightened up, surveying the garden.

"Going to be a good crop this year, I think," he said to Telos. Telos poked his head up from a few strides away, a worm wriggling from the corner of his mouth.

Chirp.

"I couldn't have said it better." Anto smiled and bent down to resume his work. Just then, a shadow fell across him.

"You missed a few weeds to your right."

Anto squinted up. Ven's smiling face hovered over him.

"Ven!"

He jumped up and gave his friend a hug out of instinct before realizing his condition.

"Oh! I'm sorry. I'm filthy and sweaty."

"I don't mind. Hi, Anto. I haven't seen you in Phrable."

Anto tried to brush dirt off his chest, managing only to smear it with his sweat into a muddy mess. "I know. I'm sorry."

"Is everything all right? When you didn't show for two weeks in a row, we got worried. Ma sent me to check in on you."

Anto shook his head. "It's Mum Gwinth. She's too weak to travel. And I can't leave her alone."

Ven's face fell. "What? What's wrong?"

He shrugged. "She picked up a rattle during the rainy season. It just hasn't left."

"Oh no! How can I help?"

Just like that. No hemming or hawing. No hesitation. Just an instant kindness.

"She would probably love to see you."

"Of course."

"Telos!" Anto called out. "Telos! We have company!"

They saw some bushes shift. Then a small head poked up. Then a crashing as the quipen raced through the grass, leaping the final few strides into Ven's arms.

"Haha. Good to see you too, Telos!" Ven laughed between licks and head rubs.

"She's probably on the porch," Anto said. "I'll be right over. Just going to clean up and put a shirt on."

"I sorta like it," Ven said shyly, giving him a look. Then he laughed and, together with Telos, went to find Mum Gwinth.

Ven spent the afternoon helping around the shop. Afternoon turned into evening then night.

"Ma knew I'd probably spend the night," he assured them. "I'll head out in the morning."

Ven's presence brought some joy back to Mum Gwinth. Never one to wallow in self-pity, she was, nevertheless, unhappy with her current inability to keep busy. She tired too easily now, able to move about for ten, fifteen minutes at most before needing to rest. They had set up a chair in the store for her to talk with customers without moving too much. The entire community was concerned but she would have none of that. She kept the store open and always had a smile to greet each and every person who walked in. Still, Anto's hope and worry were inseparable. Ven saw the stress in his friend's face and despaired.

That night, lying next to each other on Anto's bed, Ven probed his friend's feelings.

"How are you doing?" he asked gently.

In the dark, Anto could only see the shadowy bulk of Ven's body yet that was enough to comfort him a bit.

"I'm worried," he admitted. "She's not getting any better."

"She's strong."

Anto nodded. "I know. But sooner or later..."

"Hey," Ven put a hand on his arm, "she's strong. She'll pull through. And until then, I'll stay and help."

"Your family needs you."

"Ma's selling the farm."

"What?"

"Part of it, at least. She decided two moons ago. With Da gone, it's getting too much for me and Jek." He gave a quick bitter laugh. "If the crops were better, we'd have too much to do. But when they're bad, we can't make enough off of what we have."

"I'm so sorry. I should be there to help."

"You've got too much here as it is. Which is why I'm going to stay and help."

"I can't ask that of you."

"You're not asking. I'm offering."

Anto smiled in the dark. He touched Ven's arm. "Thank you."

"You'd do the same for me. Tomorrow, I'll go home and fill Ma in on what's happening. Give me a day or two to make sure Jek is caught up and I'll be back."

Anto felt a weight lifting off his shoulders. He hadn't realized until that moment just how stressed he had been with his situation. Having his friend there to help would make a world of difference. He realized his hand was still on Ven's arm, but he didn't move it. Instead, he gave a squeeze. In response, Ven stretched his top arm, pulling Anto close. Anto snuggled into Ven's chest, letting their shared heartbeat lull him to sleep.

As strong as those arms were, they couldn't protect Anto from the pain and heartache that followed. Good to his word, Ven returned a couple days later and together, they kept both the store and Mum Gwinth going. She held court from her chair at the front of the shop, although as the days grew longer, the hours she spent there grew shorter. She grew tired easily, often needing to retire to her room well before the shop closed for the day. As she faded, bit by bit, Ven and Anto grew closer than ever, brought together by their shared pain. Ven was his rock, always where he needed to be, always with a word of encouragement or a hug at the ready. Anto knew he was depending on him too much but with Mum Gwinth relying on him, he needed the support too. They formed a delicate scaffold, desperately hoping no one broke under the strain, knowing it was only a matter of time before one did.

"I'm sorry," he told Ven one night as they lay in bed.

"For what?"

"You're doing so much for me. For Mum Gwinth. You shouldn't have to shoulder this burden."

"Hey," he placed a hand on Anto's arm, "I'm here. I'm not going anywhere. We're in this together."

Overcome, Anto didn't trust himself to speak. He reached over and embraced him, expressing his gratitude with his presence.

"Thank you," he whispered into his ear, finally finding his voice.

Ven turned his head slightly until they were eye to eye. Their faces were almost touching.

Then Ven leaned in and kissed him.

It was a simple gesture. Of friendship and caring. But it had an intimacy to it that Anto had never felt before.

And, for a while, just a little while there in the dark and quiet of the night, everything was perfect.

Days stretched. Nights lingered. Crops grew and the river lowered. Then one day, Mum Gwinth reached out and took Anto's hand as he was clearing her lunch.

"Anto, sit with me for a moment."

"Of course." He pulled up a stool alongside her bed. By then, she couldn't move more than a few feet without tiring herself out, so she spent a good portion of her days in bed or sitting in her chair on the front porch.

"We must talk."

"About what?"

"About what will happen when I'm gone."

His face blanched. "You're not going anywhere."

She slowly shook her head. "We both know better."

"I don't want to talk about it." He tried to leave but her grip was surprisingly strong.

"We must. It won't be long now. I can feel Him lurking near."

"Him?"

"The Reaper."

"You're just tired. You'll feel different after a nap."

"Stop." There was iron in her voice. She only used that tone when she was angry. Abashed, Anto bowed his head, forcing himself to stop.

"I'm sorry," he said quietly.

She patted his arm. "No need to apologize. I'm not happy about it either. But we must be honest with ourselves. And prepare."

"What would you have me do?"

"The shop is yours. Do with it as you please. I will not chain you to a life you don't wish to live."

"But--"

She held up her hand. He could almost see right through it, it was so thin.

"It's just a store. Maybe Volx would take it over if you don't wish to. Or the Dungees. Or you simply close it up and move on. But do not feel like you must keep it open for me. Promise me that."

"I promise." His heart was heavy as he said the words. The thought of the shop boarded and quiet was almost too much. Mum Gwinth was the store, and the store was her. Without one, all he would have was the other. To lose both...

"And don't let Ven go," she continued. "He's a good man. And he's good for you."

Despite his sorrow, he couldn't help but smile. "He is a good man, isn't he?"

She nodded.

"You've had a rough start to this life. But those dark days don't define you. Forge your own path. Never forget but never dwell either. Do you understand?"

"I think so."

She nodded again. "Good. Now, I'm tired. I think I'm going to take a nap. Wake me for supper."

"Of course, Mum Gwinth." He bent over and placed a gentle kiss on her forehead.

As he softly crossed the room, he looked back. She had closed her eyes. She looked peaceful.

She never woke.

When Anto was nine years old:

Anto stood at the edge of the field. A line of trees ran along his right, marking the boundary between what he knew and what was unknown. He had never ventured into those trees. They were dark and held mysteries he wasn't ready to uncover.

He stood still and stared. At his feet was a rabbit. Unmoving. Dead.

It was the first time he had seen death. He couldn't tear his eyes away. The rabbit looked flat, deflated. The flies and worms obscured most of it. White bones could be seen through shredded flesh and fur.

He stared at the rabbit but didn't feel anything. There was a hole in the world right there, right where the carcass lay. Not bad, not evil, just an absence.

Later that night, by the light of the butter lamp, he tried to draw what he had seen. Over and over, he drew a rabbit, fluffy and long eared, bouncing through flowers or nibbling nervously. But nothing he drew was right. Each portrait was of something living. Mother praised his work. Father ignored him. Neither understood what he was attempting.

Frustrated, he tried again, this time drawing what he felt. Black swirls. Deep shadows. Dead eyes. Now, now he was getting closer to it. Now he was feeling along the edge of that absence.

But that was all he could do, run a finger along the edge. He couldn't capture what he had seen, had felt.

It would take many years before he became intimate with that absence.

When Anto was twenty years old:

The pyre wasn't the biggest Creekslope had ever seen, but it was the brightest. People from across the countryside came to pay their respects. To celebrate a life well-lived. Although he had only been a part of her life for a few years, Anto cried more than when he had lost his Mother. Mum Gwinth had taken him in without reservation. Had given him not just a home, but a family. And that family now gathered together to say farewell, filling the store, the yard, the field. Through a sheen of watery eyes, Anto smiled and thanked everyone, distributing and receiving hugs and handshakes. Ven and his mom and brother took care of most of the details without him even realizing it. Mar took over the kitchen, directing, organizing, cooking more food than everyone could possibly eat. Jek took command of the men, building the pyre, clearing and cleaning up the area for the guests. And Ven was there for Anto, barely leaving his side. Being steady when Anto needed someone to literally and figuratively lean on. Days passed in a blur.

The hollowness that settled in afterward was, at times, overwhelming. The store, every shelf she had built, every sign she had written, everything around him was of her. The everyday chores helped. Playing with Telos helped. Ven helped. And drawing helped. It happened almost by accident. They were eating a small supper, just Ven and Anto. As was their routine, they both cleaned up afterward, washing and drying the dishes together. A small moment, but something they both looked forward.

"I miss her," Anto said, his thoughts spilling out into the world

"I do too," Ven answered.

"I miss her more than when my Mother died."

Up to that point, Anto had said little about that time in his life. Ven glanced over at him, concern and empathy clear on his face.

"Want to talk about it?"

Anto thought about his response as he wiped a plate. Finally, he shook his head. "No. I mean, yes. I do. But I don't have the words. Does that make sense?"

Ven nodded. "Yeah. I feel like that sometimes too. Usually, I end up practicing with the bow or axe behind the barn."

"Destruction doesn't feel like the right way to express this. Mum Gwinth wouldn't want that."

"Then create something."

"I used to draw," Anto admitted. "But I was never any good at it."

Ven frowned. "What does that have to do with it? If you like to draw, then draw. Don't worry about what someone else says."

Anto flashed back to all the times Father had explicitly expressed his opinion on the subject, how he thought quite differently. He remembered trying to draw the great mountain king, Telos, only to have Father scoff and turn his face away.

"I don't know."

But Ven, being Ven, knew. The next morning, Anto woke up to find charcoals, canvases and pencils on the table. When questioned, Ven simply smiled and left Anto alone.

At first, he didn't touch the pencils. But, like an unread book sitting on the table, the pull couldn't be ignored. He soon gave in and, without really understanding what he was doing, began to put his feelings to canvas. A little at first. Just a few moments, snatched from the busy days. But then more and more. He found the time. He made the time. Drawing filled the time between chores and living. In turn, it began to fill the emptiness. Just a little.

The days grew shorter. They worked at the harvest, smaller than in years past but enough to get them through the rainy time. As his workload lessened, Anto was able to devote even more time to his art. He began to feel less empty. He tapped into his deeper self and gave it form. He gave his feelings a voice unheard but seen. At first, Ven didn't comment much on the pictures, instead allowing Anto to simply breathe into his art. But as he produced more and more, Ven couldn't help himself.

"They're beautiful."

"You're just saying that."

Ven shook his head. "I mean it. I mean, I would say it anyway because I lo—I support you. But I really mean it."

Anto stood back, critically analyzing his latest piece. It showed a flurry of wings, more emotion than corporeal. Suggestions of feathers. Hints of singing. It was divided into three areas: a light, a dark, and a neutral part, all intermingling into one cohesive work.

"You are really good," Ven said, studying the piece with him.

"Hmmm."

"What's wrong?"

Anto thought before speaking. "It's the same thing though, isn't it?" He gestured to some of the other canvases scattered about the table. "Always the same theme. Three areas."

"I did notice that."

"I don't know why I keep doing that."

"Well, what are you thinking about when you're drawing."

Again, Anto paused before answering. "Family."

It wasn't until later, when they were next to each other in bed and the night was quiet, that Anto could finally put into words what he meant.

"Mum Gwinth was like a mother to me. More than my actual mother. She took me in, cared for me, gave me a purpose."

"Is she the light in your drawings?"

He nodded. "Yeah. And Mother, my biological one, is the neutral areas. She was there, but may well not have been, you know what I mean? I remember, when I was really young, she would tuck me in and made me feel safe. But she also told me horrible things."

"Like about the Face Stealer."

"That and more. Everything she did was good mixed with bad. And, in the end, she was just there. Barely more than a spirit watching. Never active. Never doing anything. Just letting life run her over. Beaten down by the years, I guess. When she died, I barely felt anything." He turned on his side so he could look at Ven. "Does that make me a bad person?"

"No." Ven put an arm around him. "It makes you a real person. With complicated feelings."

They lay in silence for a few moments.

"Was it hard?" Ven asked. "Leaving your home?"

Anto thought before answering. "Yes. And no. Mother, despite her flaws, was the only one who saw me, you know? And when she was gone..."

"There was nothing left for you."

He nodded. "I honestly doubted anyone would even notice I was gone. Still feel that way, to be honest."

"What about the dark areas?" Ven finally asked.

The answer was easy, but saying the words was not. Anto gulped, forcing them out.

"My Father."

Once spoken, it became an obsession. Anto's thoughts turned more and more towards his Father. It was a poison, infecting his moods, keeping his memories trapped under bile and pain.

"I'm sorry," he told Ven over and over after lashing out over some trivial thing. "I don't know what's wrong with me."

"I do." Ven struggled to keep his own anger out of his voice. "Your Father. You've been thinking about him more and more lately. Why?"

Anto didn't have an answer. "I don't know. I...I guess my mind has just been thinking so much about what family means. Ever since Mum Gwinth..."

"You feel like you don't have a family anymore."

Anto heard the glimmer of hurt in Ven's voice and grabbed him in a hug. "You're my family. You know that. I know that."

Ven sighed into the hug, knowing that was true but also knowing it wasn't that simple.

"Talk to me."

And he did. Anto told him about his childhood. About the thousand thin cuts to his dignity. About the years of loneliness and feeling like nobody saw him. About trying to keep a tiny flame of hope alive in the storm.

"It was like I didn't exist. For so, so many years. I felt like I could have disappeared, and no one would have even noticed."

"That sounds so lonely."

Anto nodded. "It was. So much so that I got used to it. I didn't know any other way to live. Until I met Telos. And you and your family. And Mum Gwinth."

"You need to find him," Ven said, holding him at arm's length and locking eyes. "Confront him or forgive him or whatever you need to do. You can't just ignore this."

"No." Anto shook his head. "I don't want to see him. Ever."

"I know you don't. But you see him all the time anyway. Every time you close your eyes. You feel his presence every time you draw."

Anto knew it was the truth but the thought of being in Father's presence again chilled him.

"If only I knew he was...he was..."

"Gone?"

He nodded silently. "Then I could just walk away, knowing it was over. That he couldn't hurt me anymore."

"But you don't. And until you do, you won't rest."

Although he knew, somewhere inside, that Ven was right, it took him a few days to admit it to himself, then a few more to gather the courage to make the decision.

"I don't even know where to start," he admitted when he was finally ready.

"How about your old home?"

Anto looked at Ven sheepishly. "I don't know the name of the village. I don't know if it even has a name. It was little more than a few houses along a dusty trail. When I left, I wandered through the countryside for I don't know how long before I stumbled into your family. But I don't know which direction I had been walking or how far."

They thought about it.

"When we first met, you were surprised at how business was conducted at the market in Phrable. You said it wasn't like the market you had been to as a child."

Anto nodded. "It was a lot nosier. People yelled back and forth at each other, waving their arms and arguing."

"Let's start there then. I've only ever known the Silent Market. But maybe Ma knows about a place like you're talking about."

And so, preparations were made. The rains had slacked off and it would still be at least a moon yet before they could begin planting the spring crops. They would leave within the week. They left the shop in the care of the Dungees, a husband and wife from the other side of Creekslope. They were good people who had been friends with Mum Gwinth for decades. They were more than happy with the arrangement, having long since lost their children to disease, marriage and war. Telos sensed the start of an adventure and ran underfoot, excited and confused at all the activity. The wagon was loaded with food, bedding and tools. It was to be their home during the long days of travelling first to

Phrable then to Ven's family, then to who knew where. They had little coin but Ven assured him that they would be fine.

"Between you, me and Telos, we can figure out just about anything. Isn't that right, Telos?"

Telos chirped from atop Anto's head, bobbing up and down in agreement.

When Anto was twenty-one years old:

"A noisy market? I've heard of those."

They were seated around a large oaken table laden with food. Mar and Jek were delighted to see them and insisted on a small feast to celebrate. After a pleasant afternoon of catching up, they had spent a relaxing meal together. Only after most of the dishes were cleared and Jek dusted off an old bottle of his dad's brandy did Anto and Ven broach the subject of finding Anto's father. Telos purred contently in Mar's lap, half-asleep as she gently scratched behind his ears.

"Isn't there one south of Scada?" Jek asked.

Mar nodded. "And I think there's one west. Past the Knife Mountains."

"I don't remember crossing any mountains," Anto said. "I don't think I would have survived that, given my condition at the time."

"You were little more than skin and bones," Mar agreed.

"I remember picking you up like a sack of flour," Ven laughed. Anto blushed but probably not for the reason they thought.

"You've come a long way," Mar said with a smile. "Mum Gwinth would be proud of you."

"I know she is. I can feel her watching over me."

"But now," Ven said, "we need to exorcise this demon from his past."

"Are you sure that's a good idea?" Jek asked. "Best to leave the past buried."

Everyone looked to Anto. He lowered his eyes, hunting for the right words. "I don't know if this is a good idea," he admitted. "But I also know I need to confront him. For my peace. Not his."

"Remember that," Mar said. "Remember who you're doing this for. And why."

"I will," he promised.

"So, south?" Ven asked.

"I remember a name. Mavus? Mibas?"

"Movis?" Mar asked. "There's a small village called Movis in that direction, if I'm remembering right."

"That may be it."

She nodded. "Scada is about a two-day ride from the Silent Market. Movis is not too far from there."

"I think I can find the way from there."

"Is there a way to get there from here or do we need to backtrack to Phrable?" Ven asked.

"I think if you go due east from here, you should run across the road to Scada. But I'm not sure what the countryside is like between here and there."

"I've heard the dreadfoxes are out in numbers this season," Jek said.

"So, which route? Faster and more dangerous or slower and safer."

Ven turned to Anto. "Well? What do you think? Cross country or back to Phrable and stay on the roads?"

"Let's cut across. I want to get this over with as quickly as possible. Besides, we have Telos to protect us."

At the mention of his name, Telos raised his head and lazily looked around at them. When it was obvious no one was offering him food, he yawned and lowered his head back down to continue his nap.

Horses laden with supplies, the wagon left behind in case Mar and Jek needed it, they hugged their farewells and, with promises of staying safe, turned off the road into the surrounding country. Bow and axe were kept at the ready but there were no signs of dreadfoxes in the area. In fact, it was a pleasant ride through quiet fields and over gentle hills. They passed the time with quiet conversation and singing. At dusk, they found a sheltered spot to make camp.

"I'm worried about the horses," Anto said as they unloaded the animals.

"You worry about everything," Ven teased.

"If there's dreadfoxes in the area..."

"We'll chase them off."

Anto frowned but didn't argue. There wasn't much they could do anyway. Either they would be safe, or they wouldn't be. All they could do was take precautions and remain vigilant.

Ignoring Anto's worries, the still dusk slid into a quiet and peaceful night. Telos patrolled the edge of the campfire light, keeping them safe from any beetle or moth that wandered too close. Once, an animal stomped through the surrounding forest. Telos scampered up and around Anto until he could safely growl a warning from atop his head.

The night grew deep, and their eyes grew heavy. Finally, Ven kicked out the last dying embers and they laid down, the three of them sharing body heat to stave off the cool darkness.

"Thank you," Anto whispered.

"For what?" Ven stirred, threading an arm under Anto's.

"For coming with me. For suggesting it in the first place. For being there."

Ven laughed lightly and gave him a squeeze. "Of course. Why wouldn't I?"

Anto's hand found Ven's. "I just want you to know. I appreciate it."

"You do so much for me too. We...we make a good team."

Anto smiled in the dark. "We do."

Ven leaned forward and kissed Anto's ear.

Ven continued to speak about nothing for a while longer. Anto nodded but he really wasn't listening. He saw Ven's lips moving but the words didn't matter. He simply watched those lips, watching them in the dark. Then how his eyes crinkled in the corners. And the slight dimple on his cheek. Anto murmured "Yeah" but really was focused on how Ven moved his hands while he spoke, even lying down. And it was at the precise moment that Anto realized, that he finally admitted to himself that he was, without a doubt, madly in love with Ven.

"Did you hear that?"

Ven halted and tilted his head. Anto stopped his horse next to Ven's.

"What?"

He shook his head. "I'm not sure. I thought I heard something."

Before Anto could question further, there was a snapping of branches to their left. They were moving through a thin forest that crested a ridge. They scanned the trees in both directions, trying to pinpoint the source. But there was nothing in sight. Suddenly, a shrill shriek sliced the air. The noise pierced Anto, freezing him. But Ven reacted instantly.

"Move!" He bent over and slapped the back of Anto's horse. The horse jumped forward a second before a large body dropped from above, landing where Anto had been a fraction of a second before.

The ground shook from the impact. Another shriek as an immense bird lifted its head, throwing dirt and grass.

"Adzebeak!" Ven cried. His horse leapt forward, narrowly avoiding a slash from the creature.

The adzebeak was as tall as a man, with a heavy round body, long powerful legs ending in massive three-toed claws and a long neck that tapered to a small head with a flat, downward-curving beak. Wings that were more suited to intimidation than flight flapped wildly. The adzebeak raised its head, eyeing them with cold, ice blue eyes, its brilliant green feathers ruffled in anger. It let out another shriek and clawed the turf, readying to charge.

"Get away!" Anto called from further back. Ven struggled to right his horse and draw his bow at the same time. Seeing his troubles, Anto grabbed an axe from his saddle and leapt to the ground. His horse backed up, keeping its distance from the angry fowl.

"Hey! Over here!" Anto waved his arms, getting the bird's attention before it attacked Ven. The adzebeak turned its head, zeroing in on Anto. It shrieked.

"Come on! Come get me!"

The adzebeak ran towards him, closing the distance in three strides. It swung its head down, almost cleaving Anto in two with its sharp beak. But Anto jumped out of the way. The adzebeak shrieked again, quickly bringing its beak down again, this time catching the edge of Anto's legging.

Then it let out a pained squawk as an arrow sunk into its flank. From his horse, Ven nocked another arrow, letting it fly. The adzebeak charged Ven, reaching him before he could let another missile fly. The creature lowered its head and butted the horse, colliding hard. Ven, the horse and the adzebeak all tumbled to the ground. Ven rolled as he landed. The adzebeak brought its head down, burying its beak into the side of the horse. The horse screamed in pain. Then Anto was there, swinging his axe as hard as he could. A second later, the adzebeak fell, its breast cleaved in two.

Ven staggered to his feet. Anto was at his side in an instant, helping him.

"Are you all right?"

Ven nodded. "I think so."

A noise captured their attention. At their feet, Ven's horse struggled to breathe as its wound bled out over the grass and flowers. One look and they knew the cut had found heart blood. Grimly, Ven unsheathed his knife and did his horse one last kindness.

Anto removed the packs, transferring as much as he could to the other horse. The stench of blood and death was heavy in the air and the remaining horse stamped, wanting to leave.

"We need to clean off this blood," Anto said.

Ven nodded, looking at his soiled clothes. "The dreadfoxes will scent this in no time."

"Let's backtrack to that river we crossed this morning."

He thought for a moment. "I hate losing time, but I guess it's our best bet."

Looking around the area, Anto could almost feel hungry eyes on them. He nodded. "Yeah. Let's move."

With their lone horse laden with the extra packs, they both walked, letting Telos keep watch from the back of the horse. The horse danced about, nervous from the scent of the blood-soaked clothes. They both stripped to their undergarments to calm her, balling up their clothes and stuffing them in a pack.

"You're hurt," Anto said, eyeing a gash in Ven's side.

Ven looked down at his torso. Blood was smeared around the side of his stomach. "Doesn't look too bad."

"Let me see." Anto gently probed around the wound. It was shallow, already the bleeding had slowed.

"Will I survive, doc?"

"I think so," Anto smiled. Then he gave the cut a flick of his finger.

"Ow!"

They reached the river around midday and, after thoroughly washing, laid their clothes and bodies out to dry on a series of flat rocks.

Ven smiled as the sun warmed his skin.

"This feels nice."

Anto nodded next to him. "I hate losing the horse, though. Petal was her name. A good horse."

"A good horse," Ven agreed.

"You saved my life." Anto opened an eye and glanced at his friend.

"You saved mine," Ven responded.

"I owe you one."

"No, I owe you."

"Well, I want to thank you, regardless."

Ven turned and looked at him. "Oh? What did you have in mind?"

Anto's eyes roamed over Ven's body. "I have a few ideas."

The afternoon of that day went by in a much more pleasant manner than the morning.

"I think we're getting close to the road," Ven said late the next day. "The countryside is looking familiar."

"You think we're near Phrable?"

Ven shrugged. "South of it, yeah. I think that's the river that runs past it." He pointed to their right where, in the far distance, they saw a line of water trees. "Those look like greywood willows. They only grow along the Phrable river."

Anto grinned. "You're so smart."

Another shrug. "Pa drilled it into me and Jek to know our surroundings. He knew the fields and woods like the back of his hands."

And indeed, by dusk, just as they were searching for a place to stop for the night, they came to the road. Moving back into the bush, they went without a fire for the night, wary of cutthroats and slavers.

A strange sound woke Anto in the middle of the night. His eyes popped open, and he reached for the axe. Telos' ears perked up as well and he lifted his head, sniffing the air. He growled.

"Shh," Anto scolded.

"What is it?" Ven whispered.

"I don't know."

They lay silently, listening to the wind and the insects. Then, a moan. Muffled and indistinct.

"A person?"

"Maybe."

Carefully, cautiously, they got up and crept through the brush to where they could see the road. The moon was only half-full, so it took them a moment to spot the figure moving up the road towards them. As the figure shuffled closer, they readied their weapons. Telos growled softly from Anto's shoulder. He shushed him.

"Maybe they're in trouble," Anto whispered. "They may be hurt." They both plainly heard moans of anguish.

"Maybe," Ven conceded.

Just as Anto began to stand to offer aid, however, Ven grabbed him and pulled him down. He whispered a single word that turned Anto's blood to ice.

"Faceless."

And indeed, by the light of the moon, they could see the featureless skin of the person's head as they approached. Suddenly, the night felt colder than before. Anto almost vomited from terror. No hood covered its head. Dirty skin covered divots that once housed eyes. The middle of its face was barely more than a V-shaped ridge. Anto could see a jaw but there was no mouth to let out the moans from inside. Even the sides of their head were unsettling, having no ears to tame its unkempt hair. No way to communicate. No way to interact. Completely isolated from the world. Kept alive by the Face Stealer's cursed magic.

They watched the Faceless shuffle past, listening to the moans trapped in the mouthless head. It wasn't until it had stumbled out of sight down the road that Anto could breathe. Anto and Ven didn't speak. The unnaturalness of the Faceless stopped any words they might have spoken. It wasn't until the Faceless was out of sight that, with a shudder, they returned to camp and futilely tried to sleep through the nightmares.

"I know this place."

Anto looked around. The road wound through a forest that was becoming more and more familiar. A stump on the left. The dead ash on the right. The double dip in the road.

"Yeah?"

He nodded. "We're close, I think."

By midday, Anto was sure. With confidence came speed. They quickened their pace unconsciously, eager to reach their destination. Thoughts of what may happen were pushed aside to make room for the simple joy of returning to a place once called home. Of coming to the end of a long journey.

In the five years since he'd left, little had changed. The same-looking cattle grazed the same fields. The same houses sheltered the same people. All just a little older. Worn. Faded.

Anto's face was tight as they entered the town. His steps slowed. The anticipation of the journey's end was replaced by something else. Memories of a life thought forgotten filled his mind. Echoes of a past life filled his eyes.

When Anto was nine years old:

Anto ran. He ran to escape the yelling and crying. Ran to get away from the anger. But as fast as he ran, he still heard them. Father thundering over Mother's wailing. He didn't understand the fury of the storm, didn't know why it lived inside Father. He only knew that it hurt. So, he ran.

Thoughts of running forever consumed his mind. Just run and run and run, never turning back. Even as he thought that, though, his lungs burned, and he needed to slow down. He gulped air, hearing his heart pounding in his ears. He was near the outskirts of town, where there were more fields than buildings. The community only held about fifty families as it was. And most of those were scattered across the surrounding countryside, coming into the town proper to trade, gossip, and drink.

His family was one of the few that lived within town limits, although just barely. Now he stood at the opposite edge of town, his feet moving relentlessly.

Despite his intentions, he looked back. Towards home. Towards his family. Who were they? How did he fit in? Mother helped Lys, the loom-maker, when she wasn't taking care of the household. And Father? Well, Anto didn't really know what Father did other than lash out at those around him, either with rage like towards Mother, or with cold indifference like towards Anto.

Standing, gulping, hands on hips, Anto looked at the countryside that surrounded him. The rows of sedge. The thin creek that ran past, its location both hidden by bog heather and betrayed by bullfrogs. He thought again of running on but knew he wouldn't. All he knew was his little town. Before him lay a great wide unknown. Unknown dangers. Unknown monsters. He looked back over his shoulder towards home.

It was easier to face the terrors he knew than the ones he didn't.

Faceless   Jeff Monday

When Anto was twenty-one years old:

"Are you all right?"

Anto nodded harshly. "Yeah. Just...just never thought I'd see this place again when I left."

Ven reached over and gave his arm a squeeze.

"My--the house is past the smithy."

As they walked, Anto noticed Ven wince.

"Your side still hurt?"

Ven nodded. "A little. That adzebeak wasn't messing around."

"Let me see."

Ven pulled up his shirt. The wound was scabbed over and red around the perimeter but healing well enough.

"Well, it doesn't look too bad."

Ven dropped his shirt back down. "I'm fine. Just still a little tender. Don't worry about me."

The dusty road led them past the apothecary, saloon and goods store. They saw only a handful of people going about their business. The streets and buildings were mostly empty and quiet.

"Told you it wasn't much of a town."

"It's...quaint."

"Stop trying to be nice. This place doesn't deserve it."

"It can't be that bad. Some of these people are probably good people."

Anto grunted. But then he couldn't hold back the stress and let out a biting retort. From there, the conversation rapidly deteriorated into bickering. Anto's unease needed an outlet and Ven was the closest target. Back and forth they traded snipes as they walked down the dusty street. By the time they reached the edge of town, though, the argument had petered out. Even as they fought, both knew they really weren't mad at each other.

Anto stopped. Before them, at the end of a short yard, stood a lonely, solitary house.

Ven and Telos waited. And waited. Still Anto did not move. Telos gently stroked the hair behind Anto's ear, cooing softly in support. Ven reached over and took Anto's hand in his.

"You're not alone. Not anymore."

When Anto was twelve years old:

Anto was alone in the dark. Outside, the night was quiet and still. Father had left early in the afternoon and had not returned for supper. Mother, after a few hours, covered his plate and, after giving Anto a stern warning not to touch it, retired upstairs. Anto remained in the main room, drawing by the light of the butter lamp.

At first, he tried to draw a horse. But he couldn't get the legs right. So, he gave the horse two grand wings instead. These, in turn, grew into long, sinewy hands. Soon, he was trying to trace the shadows that flickered in the lamp light.

The night grew long. The wick grew short. Anto yawned, suddenly aware of how late it was. Even the crickets had stopped chirping. He sat up, listening to the house. Around him, just outside the small circle of light, were bumps and groans, creaks and snorts. The creatures of the night were moving about, not more than a few paces from him, separated by thin slats of aged wood. He could almost see their shadows, dark on dark, move past him, just a few steps away.

A chill took over his body and he shivered. He remembered how frightened he always got when he was younger. Back then, the night noises held unknown terrors. But now, there were plenty enough terrors inside the house. He could still hear the night noises, but he didn't call out in fear anymore. He wasn't scared of those sounds. There was no one to hear him anyway.

Eventually, he fell asleep, smudging the drawings with his cheek and drool. In the morning, he got a beating for leaving the lamp burning.

When Anto was twenty-one years old:

The house had not aged well. A heavy layer of cobwebs and dust was all that protected the worn wood from the elements, the paint long faded. One of the front shutters hung by a single nail. Bits and pieces were falling off everywhere, chipped away by rain and bug and neglect.

"It doesn't look like anyone still lives here," Ven said quietly as they stared at the house.

"No," Anto shook his head, "he's here."

"Are you sure?"

"Yeah. I can feel him." Long pause. Then he finally stepped onto the property.

Anto hesitated again once they reached the front door. Ven tied up their horse but unloaded no packs. Anto took a deep breath, and then pushed open the door.

"Father?"

The word dropped like a slug of lead in the still air.

"Father?" he repeated, taking a hesitant step into the front room. There was a noise in the back of the house. Anto and Ven looked at each other. Ven nodded in encouragement. Slowly, they made their way to the kitchen. As they approached, they heard the quiet sounds of someone chopping vegetables.

At first, Anto didn't recognize the person standing at the counter. She turned, sensing their presence.

"Oh!"

"I'm sorry," Ven said quickly, filling the silent gap until Anto could respond. "We didn't mean to startle you."

The woman, gray and weary, tilted her head, looking first to Ven, then to Anto. Her eyes lingered on him for a moment before the light of recognition sparked behind her tired eyes.

"Anto!"

"Lys?" Anto's brain scrambled to add five hard years to the loom-maker's face. Lys bustled over and gave him a hug.

"Oh, praise the gods. You've come back."

She stepped back and eyed him critically.

"You've grown."

He felt his cheeks redden. "It's been a few years."

"Aye. It has. And who's this?" She turned to Ven.

"I'm Ven." He gave a polite nod.

"And this is Telos," Anto said. Telos reached out and plucked a piece of fuzz out of her hair.

"Nice to meet you both," Lys said with a smile. "Come, sit."

Within moments, they were gathered around the kitchen table, sipping ale and searching for a way to reconnect.

"The town is quiet," Anto said, trying not to stare at the crisscrossing wrinkles that had taken over her skin since he last saw her.

"Many have moved on," she said, bitterness sitting under her voice. "Been a hard few years."

"I wasn't expecting to see you here. In the house, I mean."

She gave him a look somewhere between reproach and sympathy. "Someone needs to take care of him."

"Take care? What?"

She reached over and placed her hands over his. "Your father. He isn't well."

Anto didn't respond immediately. He didn't know what to say. He had returned expecting arguments. Fights. Yelling. Or maybe nothing more than a stone besides Mother's at the edge of the forest. But not this.

"What...what's wrong?"

"Oh, wish we knew." She blew out a long sigh that spoke of long suffering. "He came down with it oh, about a year ago. At first it was just an odd purplish sore. But it took his strength. More sores appeared. With each new one, he grew weaker. Now, he can barely move. The sores refuse to heal. None of the healers know what to do." She paused. "He's not the man you remember."

"Have others gotten this sickness?"

She shook her head. "No one else in the area."

"Why him?"

Again, she shook her head. "Only the Faceless know."

"Can I see him?"

She patted his hands once more before removing them. "He is your father, Anto. I have no place to say otherwise. But...be cautious."

She got up and busied herself with the vegetables Ven followed Anto back up the hallway to the foot of the stairs. The upper floor held only a single room: his parent's bedroom.

Anto stood at the foot of the stairs and looked up into the darkness.

"You don't have to come up," he told them.

Ven held his hand and squeezed. Telos rearranged his hair.

"Yes, we do."

With a nod, Anto ascended, purposefully stepping on the sixth step so it creaked. He wanted Father to hear them coming.

Anto pushed open the door to his parent's room. They were immediately pushed back by a wall of decay and sickness. The air in the room was almost chewable, it was so heavy. What little light that found its way through the dirty window did not to dispel the gloom but rather seemed to add to it. In the middle of the room was a bed. In the bed was something that looked like Father only in the broadest sense. His coiled muscles had melted away, leaving little but bones. Hair had either turned gray or fallen out. Whatever skin was not covered by the sheet or his shirt had oozing purple lesions. The only thing Anto truly recognized of his Father was his eyes. They were staring at him. Glaring at him. Just as hard and unforgiving as ever.

"Why are you here?" Father croaked, his voice, like his body, a mere shadow of what it once was.

"I came to see you," Anto said simply. He surprised himself by how quickly he found his voice.

"Why?"

"I--I don't know. But I had to."

"You left me." It was not so much of an accusation as a confirmation of disappointment.

Now the anger began to bubble up. Anto struggled not to yell at him. *You were never there for me! At least I waited to abandon you! I had nothing to keep me here!* So many things he wanted to say to the husk of a man in the bed in front of him. So much pain that needed to be answered for. Gods, how he wanted the man in front of him to get up out of that bed and answer for what he'd done, who he'd been. *Fight me!* A voice screamed in his head. *Fight me! Fight me, damn you! I'm strong now! I'm not a weak little kid anymore!*

But just as quickly, Anto knew it wouldn't matter. The hatred was still there. It would always be there. It was a part of him. But what was done, was done. He had a good life now. A wonderful life. Full of support and kindness. Unconsciously, he reached up and pet Telos.

And love. The love of the silly quipen on his head. And the love of the good man at his side.

"I'm here now." It was not so much of a retort as a declaration of resolve. He reached over and held Ven's hand. "What can we do to help?"

Father's eyes flickered to their hands, then away, focusing on a spot of the wall. Away from them. Looking anywhere but at Anto.

"I want nothing from you."

Whatever release Anto had been hoping for was instantly broken. Father, even in the painful throes of his illness, didn't want anything to do with Anto.

"No, I suppose you don't," Anto replied, almost to himself. "Still, I'm sure there's logs to split and repairs to be made."

Still not looking at them, Father coughed, phlegm splattering his lips and chin. "Taken care of. Neighbors."

Anto knew that was a lie. None of the neighbors had ever liked Father. Even now, with so little time left, he refused to show vulnerability.

"We'll stay the night, at least."

"No." Father's voice was flat. "No need. No room."

Despite his best efforts, Anto felt part of his heart break. That small part that he had nursed for so long, keeping it safe deep, deep inside. That part that held the last of his love for his Father. It shattered then. Shattered and fell to the unswept floor. There was nothing left to give to him. Nothing left to sacrifice.

He turned to Ven. "Let's go." Without another word, he walked out of the room.

Ven paused for a moment, then turned towards the bed.

"It doesn't have to be like this, you know. All he ever wanted was your love."

Father coughed thinly, what little of his lungs that was left barely pushing through any air.

"And all I wanted was a son I could be proud of."

"You have that. Too bad you're too blind to see."

Ven shut the door firmly behind him as he left. There was nothing more to say.

When Anto was fifteen years old:

Father was a physically imposing man. Anto knew he couldn't beat him in a fight. He could, however, beat him with words. He was smarter than Father. They both knew it. Anto tried to use his words to defend himself and Mother. Father responded with slaps and curses. He quickly learned it didn't matter how clever he was when he was on the receiving end of a belt.

"He just has a hard time expressing himself," Mother would say as they both nursed their wounds, physical and emotional.

"Why do we stay here?" Anto demanded. "Why don't we just leave?"

"And go where?"

"I don't know. Anywhere."

"Your father provides for us," Mother insisted.

"I can provide for us."

But Mother shook her head sadly. "You don't understand. You will when you're older."

"I'll never get older," he retorted. "He's killing us. He's killing you."

"Nonsense. He loves us. In his own way."

Anto tried to grab her hands but she moved away. As if any physical contact caused her pain. Anto tried not to scream at her, fought to keep the frustration from his voice.

"I'm worried. Worried about you. We're not safe here. We need to leave."

She sighed but didn't meet his eyes. "You'll understand when you're older," was her only response.

"I will never understand," he promised himself.

When Anto was twenty-one years old:

Ven found Anto outside, cold and shaking in the warm sun. He wrapped his arms around him and didn't let go until the shaking and the crying stopped.

Anto pulled away slightly so he could look Ven in the face. His eyes were puffy, but his mouth was firm.

"Thank you."

"You're a good man." Ven reached up and wiped away a tear that was rolling down his cheek. Anto leaned in again, holding Ven tightly.

"I love you," he whispered into his ear. Even though they both had been feeling that love for a while now, it was the first time either had said it out loud. Ven kissed his neck.

"I love you too."

Telos, not one to be left out, circled his long body around both their heads and cooed.

They stayed there for a moment, hugging. Then they pulled apart, kissed, scratched Telos and looked around. They held each other still, not wanting to break contact.

"I...I just...it just doesn't matter." Anto tried to explain his feelings. "He's not going to change. He doesn't care."

"And the person who cares the least always wins the argument."

"Is it sad? That even after everything, there's still a part of me that cared for him? That hurts. Why can he still hurt me? Is there something wrong with me?"

Ven shook his head. "Of course not. He's your father. He's a part of you."

"Can...I want to make sure Lys doesn't need anything. For him. He doesn't deserve it, but I have to."

With a nod, Ven led him back into the house. Lys was still in the kitchen, preparing a meal.

"Thank you," Anto told her. "Thank you for caring for him."

Her eyes, sad and tired, looked through him. "Someone needed to. After your mother passed and you left...he gave up, I think."

"He gave up a long time before that."

Lys shot him a look, torn between caring for her friend and her friend's son. "He never had an easy life, you know. He's been hurt. More than you know."

But Anto shook his head, unwilling to let that be the reason for so much suffering. "Everyone's hurt. Everyone is in pain. That's not what makes us special. It's what we do with that pain that makes us who we are."

Lys' mouth turned down into a frown and she shrugged, having nothing to say to that.

"For what it's worth, I wish things would have been different."

She nodded. "I think part of him does as well. But it's too late now. He doesn't have much time left."

"And there's nothing to be done for him?"

"No. This illness is fatal. There is no known cure."

"Is there anything we can do to help?" Ven asked.

Lys shook her head. "All I do is try and keep him comfortable."

"We can stay," he offered. "Help with chores around."

She shook her head. "It would only upset him, I think. Better to say your peace and leave him be."

"I've...I've said all I need to say." He wasn't sure if that was the truth. He wasn't sure of much at that moment, other than knowing he couldn't face those hard eyes again.

Lys nodded.

Anto placed the few coins he had on the table. "Do what you can for him. With my thanks."

She nodded and, with little else to say, they left. When they reached the road, Anto stopped and let out a long breath. But at a glance from Ven, he gave a sad smile.

"So, now what? Do you want to stay here? Is there something else you need to say to him?"

Anto shook his head. "No." He looked past the house. At the forest beyond. At the clouds. At the world outside that house. "Nothing I say will matter to him. And I've moved on. Not completely. Maybe never completely. But enough. I have you. I have Telos. I don't need him. I don't need his approval or love or acceptance."

Truly, there was a weight that had lifted from Anto's soul. He had tried to mend what had been broken. He had failed. But the act of trying gave him a lift. Lightened his soul's burden. He was sad. So very sad for what could have been. He felt the loss keenly, standing there on his Father's property. There would always be a hole in his heart.

But as deep as he felt that emptiness, he was lifted out of it. There was no more anger. No denial. Just acceptance. And with acceptance came a kind of peace.

He was broken. He would always be broken.

But he was whole as well. In his own way.

"Back home then?"

Again, Anto shook his head. Slowly, a mischievous smile crept across his face as an idea formed.

"Let's go on an adventure."

Ven laughed. For the first time in weeks, there was a spark of pure joy behind Anto's eyes. Desperate joy right then, yes. But the beginning of true and pure joy. And it made him happy.

"All right. Any ideas?"

"No. You?"

Ven grinned. "Just one. Pick a direction."

When Anto was twenty-two years old:

For six moons they wandered the countryside. They slew no dragons nor found gold, yet it was a grand adventure, nonetheless, enshrined in their memories and Ven's songlines.

One day found them camping on a high ridge, the verdant countryside laid out below them like a rumpled blanket. Telos was prowling the area, clearing away rogue beetles. Anto and Ven sat back, leaning side by side against a thick oak, enjoying the golden sun on their faces. They let the day slide by, content to sit, hand-in-hand, in silence.

"What has been your favorite part so far?" Anto asked him, eyes still closed, skin absorbing the last of the day's warmth.

"The Crystal Forest was amazing," Ven replied, his voice half remembering.

"Remember running from those Centurions in Nami?" Anto laughed.

Ven giggled. "Hey, I stole that orange fair and square!"

"They had other opinions."

"Well, you were the one who broke that wagon outside Stcharg."

"Good thing, too. Otherwise, those cutthroats would have robbed that poor family."

Ven laughed and rested his head on Anto's shoulder.

"Where to next?" Anto asked.

Ven shrugged against Anto's body. "It doesn't matter. As long as we're together."

As the sun touched the far horizon, the breeze turned cool, and they got up to start a fire. Telos stalked about, uneasy and on edge. When they settled down by the newly born fire, Telos sniffed around, unwilling to stay still.

"Telos, what is it?" Anto asked. But the quipen wouldn't settle. Instead, he whimpered and sulked. He slipped onto Ven's lap and, whimpering louder, nudged his arm.

"Hey, what's the matter, King Telos?"

Telos nudged again, growing more anxious.

"What's wrong with him?" Anto asked, a cold fear edging his heart.

"I don't know."

Telos nudged his arm again, looked at Ven with large liquid eyes, then nudged it again.

"Is there something wrong with your arm?"

Ven shook his head. "I don't think so."

Ven pulled back his sleeve. They sat in shocked silence, unable to immediately process what they saw.

"No," Anto whispered.

On his arm was an oozing purple sore.

Like those on Anto's Father.

"No. Nonononono." Anto rushed over and grabbed his arm, inspecting the lesion.

"I...I didn't know," Ven shook his head in shock.

The sore was only about the size of a fingernail but there was no mistaking it. Anto quickly rummaged around through their packs, pulling out a strip of cloth to bind it. They stared into each other's eyes, silently running through their options.

The memories of Father were still bright in their minds. Of how he was a husk of a man, in pain and unable to help himself. If this sickness could break someone like Father...

"We need to go home," Ven said after several moments. "I need to see Ma."

Anto nodded. Then he wrapped Ven in a tight hug.

"I'm not going to let this take you," he whispered fiercely, holding him as tight as he could.

"I'll be all right," Ven whispered back, a necessary lie neither believed but both needed to hear.

Anto spent the night crying into Ven's chest as they held each other. Telos wrapped his long body around Ven's neck, gently licking his hair. In the morning, they pointed their horse in the direction of home and rode. Anto was quiet, not engaging in conversation as they began the journey home. After a few hours, Ven called a halt, tired from the riding and the silence.

"Talk to me," Ven said, taking him into his arms.

Anto looked at him, eyes watery, voice fragile.

"It's my fault."

"What?"

"It's my fault. If I hadn't wanted to see my Father, you never would have gotten this."

"You don't know that."

But Anto nodded. "I do. You got the same disease. And it's all my fault."

Ven's eyes grew hard, and he leaned back, his grip on Anto strong.

"Stop. It. Stop thinking like that. This isn't your fault. This isn't anyone's fault. I wanted to go just as much as you. And maybe I would have gotten it somewhere else. Maybe I did. Only the gods know. It isn't important."

"I love you so much." Tears were flowing freely now.

"I love you too."

It took them four days to reach the farm. In that time, two more sores appeared, one on his back and another on his leg. As soon as Mar was told, she sent Jek to fetch a healer from Phrable she knew. She wasted no time in boiling poultices of herbs and minerals. Despite his protests that he was feeling fine, Ven was banned from any work. Anto, after getting scolded for hovering, kept himself busy with work around the farm, desperately yet futilely attempting to keep his thoughts from going to a very scary place.

Jek returned with the healer, Petter, near dusk. He shut them all out of the bedroom while he examined Ven. Mar busied herself in the kitchen making a meal. Jek fiddled with a frayed rope. Anto and Telos paced until Mar sent them to gather vegetables from the garden.

Finally, Petter and Ven emerged and they all sat around the table.

"Well, I'm afraid it's not good," Petter told them. "I've seen this before. This sickness has appeared time and time again. The sores will continue to appear, and his strength will wan."

"Why?" Mar asked, wringing a towel in her hands. "Why him? Why now?"

Petter pinched his nose. "I don't know. But most likely, he caught it from Anto's father."

"But I'm fine," Anto protested. "Why him and not me?"

"I don't know."

"Are we in danger?" Jek asked.

Petter shook his head. "I don't know that either. You must understand. Little is known of this condition. It affects one person but leaves the next untouched. It sweeps through a community then disappears just as quickly."

"What can we do?"

"Keep your strength up," he told Ven. "Don't overtax yourself. I would suggest keeping yourself contained to the house. Maybe that's too cautious but, like I said, we don't know much about this illness."

"That's it? Just rest and stay away from everyone?"

The healer hesitated. Anto, sensing a glimmer of hope, pounced.

"What is it? Tell us."

He hesitated. "It's probably nothing."

"Tell us."

Petter held up a hand. "It's just a thought, really. There's no guarantee it will work. Or even possible. Just something that crossed my mind the last time I dealt with this sickness."

Ven cleared his throat. "I'm willing to chance it."

"This sickness has no cure. I am sorry to say it, but it must be said. Nothing works. But maybe, just maybe, not everything has been tried. It has been long known that breathing in the fumes of a rose fire will purify the body."

Mar nodded in agreement. "Aye. That is so. The rose is the purest of flowers. Inhaling its essence cleanses the body."

"Unfortunately, this sickness is too strong for a rose fire to work. Unless..."

"Unless?"

"Unless you use a silver rose."

They sat in shocked silence for a moment. Finally, it was Mar who broke the quiet.

"Those exist only in tales."

The healer spread his hands wide. "It is the only hope I can offer. Only the rarest and purest rose can help."

"That's no hope," Anto spat. "Ven is sick, and all you offer us is a fantasy?"

Petter turned his head, letting Anto's anger wash over him. Ven placed a hand on Anto's arm, calming him.

"Are you sure there's nothing else?" Ven asked.

Petter shrugged sadly. "I'm afraid not."

Anto stood, anger and scared. "That's not enough! There has to be something else we can do!"

Heavy sigh. "If there is, only the Faceless know."

Ven found Anto out back splitting logs.

"Hey."

The axe came down hard, splintering the wood and sending chips flying.

"Hey!"

Another strike, harder than the last.

"Anto!"

Without turning, Anto buried the axe once more into the stump. "I'm not letting you go," he said.

Ven laid a hand on his shoulder. "I'm not going anywhere."

"I'm not giving up on you," he insisted.

Ven gently turned him around to face him.

"I'm not giving up either."

Both were barely able to hold the tears back as they looked into each other's eyes. A part of Anto felt like he had already lost Ven. That the man standing before him was just a ghost, a remanent of the man he loved.

"What are we going to do?" he whispered, tears flowing freely now.

"We're going to survive," Ven answered. "And we're going to live. However we can, as long as we can."

"I'm scared. I'm so scared."

"I am too."

They wrapped their arms around each other, leaning against the other, clinging to whatever hope they had in their hearts. Ven felt Anto's body against his and knew he needed to give him something to focus on, something to keep him going after losing so much.

Softly, Ven whispered into Anto's ear. "Well, let's go find a mythical silver rose."

"So. Where do we start?"

Their eyes wandered around the room, focusing inward on forgotten memories and hidden knowledge. Eventually, they settled on Mar, the most knowledgeable among them. She shifted slightly in her seat and folded her hands in front of her on the table.

"All I know is the legends," she said. "I have never seen a silver rose myself."

"That's because they don't exist," Jek spat. Mar and Anto shot him hooded looks but he shrugged. "I'm sorry, but we need to focus on what's real, not some silly children's tale."

"Legends always have a kernel of truth to them," Ven argued.

Jek shrugged again, too practical to entertain such fantasies.

"What have you heard?" Anto asked Mar. "Tell us the legend."

She sighed. "Long ago, there were two young lovers, Saffer and Ria. Saffer, eager to start a family, pleaded with Ria to give up his youthful dreams and settle down with her. But Ria, although he loved her dearly, loved adventure just as much. Many moons came and went, Ria exploring the countryside and Saffer tending the hearth. Finally, Saffer had had enough. 'I cannot wait any longer for you,' she said. 'You must choose between me and your adventures.'

"Ria's heart was torn but his love for Saffer won out. 'One more adventure,' he promised her. 'Once more into the wide open and then I will never stray from your side.'

"Although she had her doubts, she agreed. One more adventure and then they would start a family together. She watched as he packed his gear and saddled his horse. She smiled as he kissed her, though her heart was dark. She stood in the road until the sun disappeared behind the trees, looking at the path her love had taken.

"A moon passed. Then another. By the fourth moon, though, Saffer's hope wavered. She climbed the tall Cuoya tree next to their cabin, the tallest tree in the land. She wove her way through the branches until she reached the crown. From there, she looked out over the countryside, searching for a sign from her love.

"Day after day, she climbed the Cuoya, spending hour after hour among the birds and the winds, watching for Ria to return to her. And then one day, she didn't come down. The gods, in their pity, had turned her into a silver rose. A sign for her love to find her when he finally comes home."

Ven's head dropped into his hands. "In other words, the silver rose only grows at the top of the tallest Cuoya tree?"

Mar nodded. "So says the legend."

Ten minutes later, Anto was packing the saddlebags.

"What are you thinking?" Ven asked, helping with the straps.

"Cuoyas grow in the lands towards dusk," Anto replied. "I'll head in that direction. Hopefully I can find a cliff or high hill to help spot the tallest tree. It'll take some doing, but I think I can do it."

"You mean we."

Anto shook his head. "You stay here. Save your strength."

Ven grabbed him by the shoulders and turned him so they were face to face. "I'm going. End of discussion. I'm fine."

"You're not fine. I saw two more sores this morning."

Ven grimaced. "The sooner we find the rose, the sooner we can be done with this."

"But--"

Ven gave him a gentle shake. "I'm coming. Besides, if I'm with you, we can use the rose fire right away. Now stop arguing. You're wasting time."

Anto's face betrayed the struggle going on inside his head. But he finally gave a short nod and kissed him. "All right. Let's get going."

Their farewells were quick and to the point. Mar and Jek made sure they were well-supplied and before they could doubt their actions, Anto, Ven and Telos were riding towards the setting sun.

Under his breath, Ven sang a songline. Anto, lost in his fears and worries, didn't notice. Telos, riding atop Anto's head, scouted the surrounding countryside like the king he was. They rode until dusk and were on their way again at first light. Anto didn't wish to waste any time. Despite Ven's protests, Anto saw the small trembling of his hands and how he struggled to catch his breath at times. The sores, angry and purple, oozed a milky stream. Ven changed his bandages regularly, hoping to keep the infection to a minimum. They were racing against time, balancing speed with rest. And they were losing.

The hours traveling were mostly spent in silence until Ven forced Anto to talk with him.

"You need to stop this," he told Anto as they rode. "You're treating me like I'm already gone."

Anto's shoulders sagged. "I'm sorry. I'm just so...so worried."

"I am too," Ven replied softly. "But we're going to figure this out. Together. But I need you, Anto. I need you to talk to me and be at my side."

Anto looked over to him and managed a smile. "You're right. I've been in my head too much."

"Yes, you have," Ven nodded. "So knock it off."

"Yes sir."

From then, although it was difficult, it was closer to like it was in better days. They laughed and told stories. They worked together to conquer swollen rivers and fallen logs, dreadfoxes and roving thieves. Each night, they wrapped their arms around each other and kept the cold night at bay. The underlying current of fear and loss tinted everything, but they kept it at bay as best they could.

Finally, they reached the land of the Cuoya. Like giant spears thrust into the ground, the trees rose into the sky, piercing the heavens. So thick at ground level that it would take ten men to circle it, the trunks gradually tapered as they rose. Standing next to one, they felt small and insignificant compared to the ancient entities before them. They stood and peered up into the endless branches above them. The emerald canopy was high above them, impossibly out of reach and stretching on forever.

"How are we going to climb those?" Anto wondered.

"I can't even see the top," Ven added.

"And which one is the tallest?"

Ven shook his head. "Only the Faceless know."

"Maybe there's a hill or high spot of land we can look from. Get some perspective."

"I didn't see any on the way."

They stared up into the canopy in frustration. The forest was huge and imposing, with thousands of trees, each a giant. How to find the tallest among giants?

With a chirp, Telos leapt from Anto's head to the trunk of the tree.

"Hey!"

Telos scrambled up, his tiny claws easily finding purchase on the rough bark.

"Telos!"

But by the time they had dismounted, the quipen was already out of sight, swiftly climbing into the canopy. Leaves and bits of wood fell as Telos ran up the trunk.

"Telos!" Anto called. They got a faint chirp in response.

"What's that quipen doing?" Ven wondered.

Anto had to laugh. "I think he's looking for our tree. Best way to see the top is from the top, right?"

They stood at the base of the Cuoya, searching the emerald shadows above for signs of Telos. Long minutes crept past. The sounds of the birds and insects and breeze calmed their nerves as they waited. It was peaceful in the cool shadows at the foot of a giant.

Anto stepped over and slid his arm around Ven's waist, pulling him close. He kissed his neck.

"We'll find it."

"I know," Ven nodded. He leaned his head on Anto's shoulder.

Finally, they heard scratching and suddenly Telos appeared, running down the trunk like a squirrel.

Chirp. Whistle. Chirp. Chitter.

"What did you see?"

In response, Telos leapt to the ground and ran past them. He stopped and turned, whistling.

Ven quickly gathered the reins of the horses and they followed as the quipen led them through the forest. He sniffed at a Cuoya here and there, looking up and chirping. But he didn't pause long. On and on, he scampered through the forest. Once, he stopped and ran up a trunk. It was several minutes before he reappeared, chirping excitedly, and leading them on once more. Deeper and deeper into the forest they went. There was nothing but forest all around them. Anto saw no trails or tracks. The thick canopy high above kept the underbrush to a minimum. Not much could grow in such shadows. The forest was quiet, with only a random breeze to keep them company as they moved further in. It was like they were the only living creatures among the giants except for the birds that flew among their crowns. Once, twice more Telos scampered up into the canopy to check his bearings. Whistling, Telos finally brought them to a Cuoya with an extraordinarily wide base.

"This is bigger than Mum Gwinth's store!" Anto exclaimed as they walked around the massive tree. They looked up but couldn't see the top of the tree. The sheer massiveness of it was intimidating. Truly, a giant among giants.

"Is this the tree, Telos?" Ven asked.

The quipen purred and rubbed against the trunk.

"I guess it is."

Anto looked up. The lowest branch was twenty feet above them.

"No way we can jump to that."

"No," Ven answered, grabbing a coil of rope from a saddlebag. "But that won't be a problem."

Ven gave one end of the rope to Telos who scrambled up the trunk. Within seconds, he had draped the rope over the branch and brought it back down.

"I'll hold this end," Ven said. "You get to climb this monster."

Anto laughed. "Thanks." But inside, he knew Ven didn't have the strength to make the climb. He was hiding it as best as he could but there was no denying that he was getting weaker. Anto took hold of the rope, kissed Ven, and began to climb.

He pulled himself up, walking up the trunk while grasping the rope hand over hand. Telos climbed alongside him, chirping encouragement. It didn't take long before they were sitting on the lowest branch. He looked down at Ven's smiling face.

"Nothing to it!"

"How's the next part look?"

Anto gazed up at the tangle of branches above him. "Looks all right. Nothing I can't handle."

"Take the rope with you," Ven called. "In case you need it."

"All right." He hauled up the rope, coiled it and draped it over his neck and shoulder. He stood, balancing on the branch.

"Ready, Telos?"

The quipen licked his face and ran up the trunk.

"Be back before you know it!" he called down.

"Be careful! I love you!"

"I love you too!"

Anto entered a new world. A world of height rather than width. A world of browns and greens with a fleeting blue in the background. He couldn't see more than a few feet in any direction. Millions of leaves covered the surrounding world. He heard squeaks and chirps from the residents of the canopy. At first, it was easy going. Step up. Reach further. Pull. Balance. Step up. Over and over. He glanced down every so often, but the world below was quickly obscured by wood and leaf and he was left with only Telos for company.

The branches thinned as he climbed. He felt them bend under his weight. The wind picked up as well. Although he couldn't see the ground, the feeling of being suspended high above the world was overwhelming. He clutched the trunk of the Cuoya, keeping his weight as close to the base of the branches as possible. Next to him, Telos whistled encouragement. He ran up and down the trunk, chattering excitedly as if telling Anto how much further he needed to climb.

Eventually, he reached a point where the branches were too small to support him. He looked up. The leaves were thinner now. He saw more blue between the green. He was near the top. A breeze came past, and he swayed with the tree, holding tightly as his world bent.

Telos whistled from above his head.

"I can't go any further, Telos," he said. "The branches won't support my weight. Can you see the rose?"

Telos scrambled up. A moment later, the quipen chittered excitedly and ran back down to him.

"Can you chew through the stem?"

Telos ran up. But he returned with no rose and a nasty scratch across his nose.

"Oh! The thorns, huh?"

Telos purred and nuzzled Anto's ear.

"All right. Give me a moment."

Holding tightly as the tree swayed, Anto tried to think of a solution.

"Telos, will the rope reach the base of the flower?"

Telos tilted his head, then chirped. Anto uncoiled the rope and gave an end to Telos who clamped his jaw around it.

"Take this and wrap it around the base of the flower, just like with the branch at the bottom when we started."

Telos ran up the trunk, dragging the rope after him. Anto tied his end around the tree. Once Telos returned, Anto slowly pulled, bending the top of the tree towards him. Bit by bit, he pulled. It was difficult to keep his balance so he stopped and sat, wrapping his legs around the branch he was on and wrapping the rope around the trunk so he could pull easier.

"Telos, tell me when it's in reach," he said. He strained as he pulled, concentrating on keeping his balance. The top of the tree bent over him. Bits of wood fell on him. The rope was tight. His arms shook with effort. Finally, Telos chirped excitedly. Holding tight, Anto glanced over his shoulder and saw it! Bent almost upside down a little over an arm's reach away, was the most beautiful flower he'd ever seen. Its petals shone a brilliant silver in the dappled light. There was no mistaking it for metal, however. Even the most casual glance told of its natural softness. It was large, bigger than his hand, with thorns that looked like they would puncture clean through his arm. No wonder Telos wasn't able to chew through the stem. *Such a thing could only be the work of gods*, he thought, he breath unconsciously held in his

throat as he stared at it. Carefully, Anto tied off the rope. The
rope quivered with tension, ready to snap back at the slightest
mistake.

"Stay away from the rope," he warned, "in case it breaks."
Telos moved around the trunk, peering from the other side.
Moving very carefully, Anto got to his feet and shimmied along
the branch. Less than the width of his foot, it bent as he moved
forward. He reached up and grasped the branch over his head for
stability. Holding onto the branch with one hand, he stretched his
other, just touching the rose stem. Thorns like daggers bounced
as the rope quivered. The stem was too thick to snap. He slowly
brought his hand away and grabbed his knife. Again, he
maneuvered his hand between the thorns and slowly sliced into
the thick woody stem.

Each time he applied pressure, the rope vibrated, ready to
snap. He couldn't move closer without breaking the branch he
stood on. Gritting his teeth, he sawed at the stem, slowly running
the blade back and forth, digging into the fibers. Thorns
scratched his hand as he worked, despite his caution. Soon,
blood flowed from multiple wounds, but he ignored the pain and
sawed.

Just when the tension was at its breaking point, when he
heard the branch crack under his feet, his knife cut through the
last of the stem and the silver rose dropped. Anto moved back,
sighing heavily. He looked down, spotting a flash of brilliance
among the leaves below.

"Telos! Find the rose!"

Telos barked and scrambled down the trunk, on the hunt.
Anto glanced back at the tree tip. His eyes grew wide for, even
as he watched, the stump sprouted a bright green shoot. Before
his eyes, a new, lustrous flower bloomed, becoming whole once
more. The part of Anto's heart that had been torn by the thought
of destroying something so unique and beautiful relaxed at the

sight. The silver rose was eternal. It must be the cure! Only something as wondrous and magical as this could cure Ven.

A thought crossed his mind. Perhaps he could cut another rose. Better to have more than one, just in case. Gingerly, he scooted his foot forward, trying to hang as much of his weight on the branch above as possible. A loud crack sounded, and he felt his body shudder. Grimacing, he moved back towards the trunk. The branch cracked again. Even next to the trunk, his weight was too much for the weakened branch. It would surely break if he stepped out on it again. One rose would have to be enough.

Quickly, he untied the rope and eased the top away. He pulled on the rope, but it snagged and wouldn't come free. He would have to leave it. Without Telos, there was no way to retrieve it. He carefully lowered himself to the next branch, only letting out the held breath when he was safely climbing down.

A moment later, he saw a flash of light. Telos was walking along a branch a few feet below him, the silver rose daintily held in his mouth.

"Well done, Telos! Take it to Ven. I'll be right behind you."

Telos chirped around the stem and scampered away. It didn't take long before Anto was once again on the lowest branch. Below him, Ven grinned up at him.

"Am I glad to see you!"

"Easy as falling off a log," Anto joked. "But I had to leave the rope."

"There's another in the pack. Hang on."

"Funny."

Ven got the other rope and, again with Telos' help, looped it around the branch so Anto could repel down to solid ground and a fierce hug from Ven.

"I kept expecting you to fall out of the sky."

"Almost happened once or twice," Anto admitted.

Ven hugged him again, shaking from stress and exhaustion. Then they quickly made a fire. Once the blaze was going, Anto followed Mar's instructions. He took a single, brilliant leaf from the rose and placed it in one of their metal camp cups with a little water. Then Ven bent over the cup and Anto placed a cloth over his head. Ven inhaled the steam of the boiling rose water, breathing deeply its purifying fumes. Only once the water had boiled away and the leaf was less than ash did Ven emerge from under the cloth.

"Well? How do you feel?" Anto asked anxiously.

Ven took a deep breath, expanding his chest as far as he could. He slowly let it out. Turning to Anto, he smiled.

"Good. Better."

"You're not just saying that?"

Ven laughed and Anto could hear the honest joy. "No. I really do. I mean, I still ache everywhere, but..." He held out his hand. The trembling wasn't as pronounced. "...better."

Anto breathed a long sigh of relief. They checked his body constantly for the next several hours. No new sores formed, but the old ones didn't go away either. The oozing lessened but did not stop. Even the power of a silver rose fire could only halt the illness, it seemed.

"It's not working," Anto slumped his shoulders. "Gods, it's not working."

"It's helping," Ven replied, examining a sore. "Maybe it just takes more time to work."

"Maybe."

"I bet it just takes a couple treatments."

"We only have the one rose," Anto protested. "We have ten, twelve petals. That's it."

"Then that will be enough," Ven announced, false confidence in his voice.

"And if it's not?"

"Then we try something else. At least it's halting the sickness. That gives us time."

It wasn't a cure. They knew that. But it was something positive. There was still hope.

The journey home was not rushed, yet they dared not linger. With only a single silver rose to stave off the sickness, they needed to find a permanent cure quickly. Despite that, they enjoyed the moments they shared, knowing their time together was more precious than ever. At every village and town they passed through, Anto spoke with every healer and wise woman but, though all knew of the sickness, none knew of a cure.

"We'll find something," Ven said one night as they sat together next to a small fire. Anto absently stroked Telos' fur while the curled up quipen slept in his lap.

"I know," he sighed. "It's just so frustrating."

"There has to be something. We just have to find it."

Anto shot him a smile. "We will. I swear it."

"Until then," Ven reached over and took Anto's hand, "please, let's make the most of the time we have."

"We have until the end of time."

"Until the sun burns out," Ven said grandly.

"Until the rivers dry up," Anto shouted.

"Until the mountains crumble," Ven sang.

From his lap, Telos grunted, annoyed at the commotion.

"Until quipens don't need seventeen naps in a day," Anto laughed.

Telos playfully nipped at his hand and they laughed some more.

By the time they reached home, half of the rose had been burned. Ven was feeling strong. Stronger than he had in a while. But the lesions did not heal. While they had been gone, Mar and Jek had talked to everyone they knew throughout the countryside. Various balms and salves were suggested and tried. But only the fumes of the silver rose had any effect on the illness.

Anto, frustrated and scared, split his time between hovering over Ven and wandering the nearby towns for information. Again and again, Ven had to plead with him to just be there.

"You're obsessing," he scolded.

"Of course I am!" Anto snapped back. "The rose is almost gone. We're running out of time."

"No," Ven shook his head. He grabbed Anto by the shoulder and locked eyes with him. "I'm running out of time. You're not. You need to come to terms with that."

"No!" Anto tried to pull away but Ven held fast.

"Yes. Promise me you'll let me go, when the time comes."

"You know I can't do that."

"You have to."

Anto shook his head but still Ven refused to let him go.

"Anto. Anto, look at me. It's all right. It will be, I promise. But only if you let me go."

"No. I can't." He buried his head into Ven's shoulder. "I can't lose you."

"We'll meet again. When your time comes, I'll be waiting for you."

Tears spilled out of his eyes but Anto didn't wipe them away, letting them soak into Ven's shirt. He held him tightly, not wanting to let ever let go.

"There has to be a way," he whispered.

Anto watched as Ven breathed in the last of the silver rose fumes. Immediately upon their return home, Mar had taken a cutting from the base of the woody stem in the hopes of growing a silver rose of their own, but it came to naught. Now, it was all gone. From then on, Ven's condition rapidly worsened. The sores spread, oozing his life away. His once solid muscles melted from his body, leaving him thin and weak. His face sunk. His once strong jaw became sharper, covered only by an increasingly thinned layer of skin. Within a fortnight, he was spending most of his time in bed, frustrated yet helpless.

Telos refused to leave his side, much like when Mum Gwinth took ill, giving him what comfort he could. Jek, stoic as ever, worked from before dawn until long after dusk, taking care of all the chores and freeing Mar and Anto to care for him. Anto kept up a brave face in front of Ven but broke down into tears whenever he left the room. He felt so powerless.

"Is there anyone else we can talk with?" he pleaded one night. He was sitting with Mar at the table downstairs, neither eating.

Mar shook her head. "I don't know. I can't think of anyone."

"There has to be a cure! There has to be!"

"If there is, only the Faceless know," she lamented.

Only the Faceless know.

An expression he'd heard his entire life.

A phrase that held so much horror.

But.

But also, a promise.

"Only the Faceless know," he repeated quietly. There must have been something in his voice because Mar looked up sharply.

"No, Anto." She shook her head violently. "No."

"What other choice to we have?"

"That is no choice!"

"They know the cure. They know all."

"But the price. The curse. Even if you found them, what good would it do? You'd be cursed to wander the land forever."

"The legend says that if you find a way to use the knowledge you gain, the curse is broken, and you regain yourself."

"How?" she demanded. "How can you use the knowledge if you can't speak. If you can't see or even hear?"

"I don't know," he admitted. "But there has to be a way."

"You've seen the Faceless. You've seen them trapped in their heads. No," she insisted. "This is not the answer."

"Then what? What else can we do?"

"We will find a way."

"Ma, we both know there is no other way. Hells, we tracked down a mythical rose and that didn't work! What other option do we have? The Face Stealer knows all. I ask them a question and they tell me. As long as I can use that information, I break the curse and Ven is cured."

"I have never heard of someone breaking the curse. So many have tried. None have succeeded."

"I don't care. I have to try."

"And leave Ven?" Her eyes pleaded with him. "And not be here when he needs you most?"

Anto looked away. "I have to try, Ma. I have to. I can't let him just fade away."

"It's too great a gamble."

"It's worth it. For Ven."

She sighed heavily. They sat in several minutes as Mar fought with herself. Anto was as well. What he was proposing was certain death. No. Worse than death. An eternity of wandering the land, helpless.

"I can't let you do this," she said quietly but firmly.

Anto struggled with his emotions. He wanted to stay. More than anything, he wanted to stay at Ven's side and believe he was going to recover. He needed to go. He couldn't watch his love fade away. Ven needed him to stay. He needed him to find an answer. Eyes full of tears, he looked up and into Mar's weary and frightened face. She was losing her son. Now he was asking her to let him go as well. To condemn himself to a fate worse than death.

"All right. I'll stay." They both hoped it was the truth. They both knew it was a lie.

She nodded and wiped away a tear.

Ven stirred, his sleep restless. Anto dabbed at his forehead with a cool rag, clearing away the sweat and cleaning the sores as best he could. Ven's eyes fluttered but didn't open. Anto watched him as he slept, taking in every detail. His stubble, how his mouth parted just a little as he slept, everything from his eyebrows to the mole on his cheek. He wanted to remember. He needed to keep Ven's face in his memory. He shivered, thinking he may never see it again. He reached out and gently caressed Ven's cheek.

Little pup, little pup

Where have you gone?

The sun is going down

Oh, little pup, come home.

Anto sang quietly around his tears, remembered when they had first met all those years ago.

"I have to go away for a while," Anto said softly. His eyes drank in Ven's face, burning it into his memory for when he would have no sight. "I have to go, but I'll be back, I promise."

Telos rubbed up against his arm, whining.

"No," Anto shook his head, petting the quipen. "You can't come with me. I need you to stay here and watch over him for me, all right?"

Growling, Telos nipped at his hand.

"I'm sorry." Anto pet his head. "I'm so sorry. But I need you to stay here. I need to know you're taking care of him for me."

Telos wound his way through Anto's arms, nuzzling his cheek and licking his ear. Anto hugged him tightly for several moments, wetting the quipen's fur with his tears.

"Please, take care of Ven until I get back."

Telos cooed, then crawled back over onto the bed, snuggling up to Ven's side. Anto leaned forward and kissed Ven.

"I love you."

Wiping away the tears, Anto left the room before his resolve dissolved.

"Take Jek with you. He can at least guide you back to us."

Anto turned. Standing in the doorway, framed by the morning sun, stood Mar. Her face showed resignation and sadness.

Anto shook his head. "No. You need him here. And the legend is clear. Only those seeking wisdom may approach. Remember?"

She nodded.

" 'Stout of heart, seekers of mind,

Come to us and you will find.

But the path is yours and yours alone,

All others will turn to ash and bone.' "

They were silent for a moment, pondering. Mar looked at him, her face crushed with loss.

"What shall I tell him?"

Anto blinked back tears, the weight of life pressing him down. "Tell him...tell him I'm getting a cure. Tell him to hold on. To wait for me to return. Tell him not to give up."

She reached out and held his hand tightly. "You come back to us," she told him. "You come back to us and we'll take care of you."

"I will. I will find a way."

They hugged fiercely, crying into each other's shoulders. Finally, Anto gently pushed her away and got on his horse. Anto pointed Pearl towards the dark mountain in the far distance and departed. Immediately, guilt almost made him turn back. Guilt at leaving Ven. He should be at his side, comforting him until...

He shook his head. That was why he had to leave. He had to find a cure. And there was only one way of doing that. He sat up straight in the saddle, pretending he felt brave and confident. But he didn't. He was scared. More scared than he had ever been before. Scared and alone once more.

To make himself feel better, to feel like Ven was at his side once more, Anto began a new songline. He sang about the trees he passed and the rivers he crossed, the hills and valleys and turns. Verse by verse, he built a songline, feeling Ven near his heart. So passed a day and a night and another day.

The world grew decrepit the closer he got to the home of the Face Stealer. The air became cold and biting. It burned his lungs when he breathed in. Vegetation turned brown and sickly. Flowers that were normally benign dripped toxic goo. His horse whinnied, nervous and skittish.

He passed a Faceless a full day's ride from the mountain. Then another by dusk. Before he reached the foot of the mountain, he had seen well over a dozen. All shuffling around, lost and cursed, unable to find their way.

As he rode, he sang his songline. Maybe, just maybe it would guide him back home. If he could remember it all. He again thanked Ven for staying with him, even if only as a song.

He spotted a flash of white, just past the treetops. Slowing, he rounded a bend in the road and stopped. Before him was a beautiful white structure. A steeply-steepled roof ended in a sharp point at the top. Unadorned and windowless, the church had an odd feel to it. He dismounted and tied Pearl to a nearby tree, his curiosity piqued.

"Hello?" he called as he approached. He thought he heard moaning coming from inside, but the wind and the wood made it too difficult to know for sure. He called out again at the door. Tentatively, he reached out. With a click, the door swung open.

Although it was sunny and warm outside, the interior of the church was dark and cool. He heard moans. He smelled unwashed bodies. As his eyes adjusted to the shadows, he realized there were bodies sprawled out throughout the room. Each person wore a white robe in varying states of filthiness. Each laid about as if in pain.

Each was Faceless.

They shifted and clawed at one another. Or sprawled out on the floor. Or slumped against the wall. Each trapped in their own heads. Each in a personal hell. Their moans filled Anto's ears. His brain could barely process the writhing mass of limbs in front of him, featureless and nameless. Nothing more than arms and legs and torsos moving back and forth in a hopeless fugue.

Eyeless heads swiveled on thin necks, seeming to stare at Anto from the gloom.

He stepped back in horror and bumped into something. Whirling, he saw a priest standing next to him.

"Easy, weary traveler," the priest said with an oily voice. His face was long and creased with age, but his eyes glinted in the dull light of the church from an inner fire that unsettled Anto. His robes were clean and mended, a sharp, bright white among the shadows and dirt of the church interior.

"Who are you?" Anto demanded. "What is this place?"

"This place? This is the Church of the Faceless."

"Oh!"

"Have you come to join the movement?" The priest took a small step forward, a hand reaching out.

"No! I mean, no. I was passing through and was curious."

"Ah." He dropped his hand. "But surely, if you're passing through, you are a Seeker, are you not?"

"I'm...my business is mine."

"True," the priest nodded. "Yet we are all united in our desire to learn."

"Uh...sure."

"Do you know anything about the Church?"

"Honestly? Not really."

"Come," he smiled coolly, "let us sit in the sun and I will explain."

Unsure yet not feeling threatened, Anto followed. The priest sat on a fallen log just to the side of the church. Anto, after checking on Pearl, stood near.

"The Church of the Faceless is dedicated to learning the Truth," the priest intoned.

"What truth?"

"Why, the reason, of course. The reason for all of this." The priest waved a hand around. "The purpose of life. The meaning of existence. The Truth."

"I see."

"Our congregation leads the way to the Truth." He looked up, beaming in the sun.

"How do they do that?"

The priest blinked his pale eyes at Anto. "Why, by asking the Question, of course."

And then everything began to click into place in Anto's head. "I understand. You send these poor people to the Face Stealer, hoping to get the answer to your 'question' without putting yourself at risk."

"No, my son," the priest shook his head. "Our congregation willfully approaches the Sage One. They then return to us to share their knowledge. Only together may we move forward."

"But if they shared their knowledge, the curse would be broken. Yet I saw dozens of Faceless in your church."

"Alas," he sighed, "it is rather difficult to convey wisdom. But we are dedicated to work together until we are all enlightened."

Anto felt a sour taste in his mouth. He shivered despite the sun. "I should strike you down right here, so you don't entrap any more innocents in your lies."

"I am but a servant to a higher power," the priest responded, unconcerned with Anto's threat. "There are many servants in this world. I am but one."

Anto knew what he said was true. He had seen many priests over the years in Phrable and other towns. Killing this man wouldn't solve anything. People would always be willing to sacrifice themselves for a cause, even if that cause was foolish. How many times had he seen these acolytes in Phrable and other towns? They were everywhere.

Nothing would be gained by killing this priest. Another would simply replace him. Yet how could he simply stand by and let him sway others to walk such a dark path?

"But if I kill you here, at least I save those who will be coming after me past this spot."

The priest nodded. "For a time, yes."

Anto's hand drifted to the knife at his waist. The priest's eyes flickered to the weapon, then back to Anto's face.

"If you truly wish to strike me down, I will not resist."

Through the open door of the church, Anto heard the moaning of the Faceless within. So many people willing to throw their lives away. For what? At least he had a purpose, a reason for his sacrifice. What purpose did they have?

As if reading his thoughts, the priest smiled. "Who are you to question the path of another?"

Disgusted, Anto walked away. There was no winning here. Nothing he could do to help those inside or those that would come after. And he had his own purpose. He untied Pearl and led her away from the priest and the moans and the smug righteousness of a zealot.

He reached a spot where the shadow of the mountain let no sunlight touch the ground. Pearl stamped and snorted, adamant about turning back.

"I'm sorry," he told her. "I have to continue."

But she planted her hooves and tossed her head back and forth. Sighing, Anto got down. He rummaged through his provisions, stuffing his rucksack with a blanket and a canteen filled with just enough water for the journey to the top. Then he ate his fill, sharing with Pearl. He would have no need for food once his mouth was taken but the extra energy would be crucial so he ate all he could.

"I'm not asking you to wait for me," he said to Pearl, feeding her an apple. "Stay safe. Find your way home, if you can."

He gave her a pat, a hug, and then a smack, sending her back up the trail. He watched as she trotted off, leaving him alone with only the dust she had kicked up. Turning, he eyed the dark mountain that rose before him. A shudder ran through his body, ice-cold and the first of many to come.

The path before him looked different. Shrubs and ferns were more yellow than green. Trees were sickly and thin. Even the air seemed to take on a yellowish hue. It was if someone had drawn a line across the land; one side was lush and green, and the other was stunted and twisted. Anto saw a pile of ash, just past the boundary. He saw a glint of metal. Buttons. Like someone's jacket had burned up. He shuddered, knowing there had been a person in that jacket. Someone who had tried to turn back after setting foot in the Face Stealer's territory.

Anto hesitated, knowing this was his last chance to turn back. The lore was clear. 'Step foot on my mountain only you who seek.' He thought of Ven. Strong, healthy, beautiful Ven. His smile. His laugh. His singing. He would do anything for that man. Even so, he hesitated, the weight of what he was about to do almost crushing his resolve. If he took another step, he was dooming himself to a living hell. Breaking the curse would be practically impossible. He would lose Ven forever. He would lose his entire world.

But he was going to lose Ven anyway. He needed to save him. He needed to try.

He imagined what Ven would say to him, if he was there right at that moment. He would tell Anto he wasn't worth it. That life would continue once he was gone. And it would. But it wasn't a life Anto wanted to live.

He felt all the loss and suffering of his life up to that moment. All the pain and loneliness. Ven was the opposite of all that. He was love and caring, understanding and laughter.

As he stood there, on the edge of eternal suffering, he knew that he wasn't doing this just for Ven. He was trying to make sense of his life, of giving his life some purpose other than suffering. He was praying this act of sacrifice would balance out all the horrible things.

If Ven died, he would die as well. Whatever shards of his heart were still within him would shatter and he would be nothing but a husk. *If I'm going to die,* he thought, *let it be on my terms. Let it be for love.*

Anto looked up at the blue sky above him. At the green and brown trees around him. He listened to the birds and felt the wind.

Such a beautiful world, he thought, soaking in as much as possible. *So beautiful.* He inhaled deeply, steeling his nerves.

And then, he stepped forward. Jaw set. Eyes locked on the path ahead. He would cure Ven. He would find the way back to him.

Mere moments later, he came across a Faceless. They were lurching back and forth, wildly flailing in a desperate attempt to escape the mountain. Anto was forced to step off the trail lest they collide with him. Burrs pricked his skin as he pushed further into the brush. The muffled screams of the Faceless were pitiful and heart-wrenching.

The next Faceless he encountered was simply standing in the middle of the path. Anto watched as they turned their featureless head, trying to sense which direction to walk.

"This way," Anto said out of habit. Steeling his nerves, he approached them. He reached out cautiously, intending to steer them down the mountain. But the moment he touched them, the Faceless jumped back, swinging fists wildly. Anto barely ducked a blow. The Faceless moaned and stumbled off. There would be no helping them. There would be no help for him.

Softly, he sang the songline, building it verse by verse, counting paces, ignoring visual cues:

"Thirty paces then a slow left arc,

Stay to the right, feel for the bark

Of an ash, an oak, then 'nother ash..."

He encountered more Faceless as he climbed. Some stumbled forward. Some sat, their useless heads hanging between knees. Others lay on the ground, asleep or simply refusing to move. It took half a day to reach the summit. What little vegetation clung to the rocks was dry and brown, dead yet refusing to blow away on the constant bitter wind.

Every so often, he spotted a pile of ash. Or the burned remnant of a sleeve or boot or bone. Nothing was left of those that turned back except charred leather and ash. Constant reminders to continue forward. He couldn't turn back. Behind him was certain death. In front, a living hell.

The trail was steep but ran true. The trees and bushes grew thinner as he climbed, and the wind grew stronger. A bitter and cold wind. He wrapped his coat tighter and kept his eyes forward and his feet moving. If he stopped, he didn't know if he would have the strength to start walking again. Finally, he crested a large incline and stopped short. He blinked, unable to believe the sight before his eyes.

Perched on the edge of the mountain was a prim, tidy chalet. Its door and shutters were painted a deep emerald. Its wooden walls were stained cherry red. The area around the chalet was clean and swept, with two well-manicured firs flanking the small porch. From the brick chimney, a thin line of white smoke rose, instantly taken by the mountain winds. It looked cozy and welcoming and warm.

"Not exactly what you were expecting, is it?"

Anto whirled around, startled by a voice after so long of seeing heads with no mouths. Sitting on a large rock just off the path was a young woman. Long strawberry blond hair framed a sun-worn and freckled face. Her clothing, a simple brown traveling outfit, was in good repair and mostly mud-free. She was sitting with her hands clasped between her knees. Her expression was long yet managed a thin smile.

"Who are you?"

She shrugged. "Does it matter? Soon, you won't be able to recognize me anyway."

He thought about it for a moment. "I don't believe that," he finally replied. "I have to believe we're more than our physical features."

She smiled an extraordinarily sad smile. "Maybe."

He sat down a dozen paces from her. They both spent several minutes staring at the chalet, thinking about their immediate future. Finally, the inevitable question crossed his lips.

"What are you going to ask them?"

She laughed bitterly, then said three words he was not prepared to hear.

"I don't know."

His jaw fell open.

"What? How?" His mind couldn't process it. To sacrifice so much for...nothing?

She shrugged. "I thought I knew. I thought I needed an answer that was worth it. But I guess I've realized I never needed that answer. So now I'm trying to figure out what question to ask."

"I...I don't know what to say."

She shrugged again. "Not much to say. I was foolish. I know that now. And now," she gazed at the chalet, "now I have to pay for my folly."

"Unless you get the answer to a question that will make it all worth it," he pointed out.

Another bitter laugh. "Like what? What is the meaning of it all? Will I be missed?"

"Something. There must be something."

"What about you?" she asked suddenly, obviously needing to change the subject.

"I...the man I love is sick. He has an illness, and no one knows how to cure it. I'm here to find out how to save him."

"You'd give up your life for him? Knowing you'll never see him again? Hear him?"

Anto nodded. "I have to try. If I fail, he will die soon. If that—I won't let that happen. I won't."

Again with the sad smile. "I used to feel that way about someone once."

"What happened?"

"His love wasn't as deep as mine."

"Is that why you're here?"

She nodded. "I was hurt. I wasn't thinking clearly. I wanted to know why he didn't, couldn't love me like I loved him. I was in such pain. Have you ever had your heart broken? It is the worst pain in the world, I think. I couldn't stop crying. Nothing mattered. I couldn't eat, couldn't sleep. I just wanted to die. Even more, I wanted to know. Wanted to know why. Why couldn't he love me? What was wrong with me? What was wrong with us? But once I was on this cursed mountain, I came to realize it didn't matter. He just didn't matter. The why just doesn't matter."

"How long have you been sitting here?"

"Two days," she admitted. "I've survived off of food from the packs of other pilgrims, abandoned after they're...taken."

"I'm so sorry."

"Don't be. Pity won't help me."

"It's not pity," he insisted. "I truly am moved by what you've been through."

"Thank you. That is kind. Useless, but kind."

He looked again to the chalet, seeing only Ven. He reached into his pack, but he had nothing to offer her other than a few drops of water at the bottom of the canteen.

"Here. I wish I had brought more."

"So, you're going in?"

He nodded. "I have to. Ven grows weaker every hour."

"I hope you find the answer you seek."

"It's not the knowledge I'm concerned with," he replied. "It's using it."

He stood, brushing off his pants. "If you're still here, when I come out, would you mind turning me in the right direction?"

"Of course."

He nodded his thanks and took a step forward, his foot leaden. Then another. The chalet filled his vision. Under different circumstances, he would have appreciated the fine craftsmanship of the building. Great skill was evident in every detail, from the sturdy posts to the intricate, elegant carving of the trim. But those fine touches served only to increase his unease. Knowing what was to happen to him inside made the artisanship perverse and unsettling. The many piles of ash scattered about the entrance didn't help either. So many people, who braved so much, only to lose their nerve at the last moment. Now they were bits of carbon, floating on the wind.

He stopped at the door, unsure if he should simply enter or knock first. But the door opened before he could lift his hand, swinging silently on well-oiled hinges. Anto took a deep breath and stepped over the threshold.

The front room was open and spacious. A large fire blazed in the fireplace, filling the room with cozy warm air. The wooden floor, waxed and shiny, peeked out from beneath a multitude of rugs. Plump chairs and tidy tables dotted the room.

Lace curtains framed cleaned windows, letting in soft sunlight. From another room wafted the scent of freshly baked bread. The place felt like an estate house of the gentry, exceedingly comfortable and insulated from the worries of the world.

Anto looked around, finally spotting a small figure sitting in a chair near the fire.

"Hello."

"Sit with me," the figure said, his voice warm and inviting. "You must be tired after such a long climb."

Anto crossed the room and took a seat opposite the man. Although man was not, perhaps, the best term to describe the creature before him.

He had a large head, much larger than proper for a human, with pointed features; ears, nose, chin, and teeth all ended in sharp angles. His skin was a pallid yellow, yet he appeared to be in excellent health with not so much as a polite cough interrupting his speech. His eyes were the opposite of a man's, black sclera, green iris and white pupil. He was impeccably dressed in fine maroon silk and white ruffles. He sat with a leg crossed over the other, showing a black-haired leg where his pant ended and a hoof like a goat. Everything about him was refined, elegant and menacing. His unsettling eyes took in Anto in an instant, appraising him. Judging him perhaps.

"Ah, good. You are not of the Church."

Anto shook his head. "No. I'm not."

The creature grimaced in disgust. "Poor, misguided souls, thinking the answer to the Question is the same for everyone."

Anto did not respond, his mind instead racing as fast as his heart.

"I am the Comte Visage," the creature said, taking a sip from the cup on the table next to his chair. "And you are?"

"Um, Anto. I'm Anto."

The Comte smiled, his sharp teeth glinting in the firelight. "Pleased to make your acquaintance, Anto. Something to drink? Brandy? Ale?"

Confused and nervous, Anto shook his head. This was not what he had expected.

"You were assuming I would live in a cave, perhaps?" The Comte laughed lightly, recognizing the confusion writ plainly on Anto's face. It was a pleasant laugh which made it all the more unsettling. "Dressed in rags and surrounded by the bones of my victims?"

"Um, yes. Something like that," Anto admitted.

"Oh, I'll be honest, when I first began this enterprise, it was a rather small endeavor. But over the years, I have been able to capitalize on my success. I am a firm believer in reinvesting in my business."

"I..see. How--?"

The Comte held up a hand, long and pointed. "I must caution you, dear boy. The terms are rather clear. You are entitled to one question and one question only while in my presence. Do not waste it."

Anto took a breath and gathered his thoughts. "I assume, by the look of your house, that you have been doing this for some time."

The Comte nodded. "A little over three hundred years. Are you sure you don't want anything? Tea, perhaps?"

He shook his head again. "No, thank you."

"Right. To business then. How can I assist you?"

"First, a couple ques—I mean, I am concerned about a few things."

"Oh, by all means, continue." The Comte clasped his hands over his knee, relaxed and in no hurry, his toothy smile unnerving Anto.

"It is said you know everything."

The Comte nodded. "I am what you might call an 'information broker.' My sources are impeccable."

"One would naturally worry about the accuracy of the information."

"And one would be prudent to do so. However, you have my personal guarantee that the information I provide is completely accurate and reliable. Satisfaction guaranteed or double your face back." He broke out into a chuckle at his own joke, again showing his very pointy teeth.

"So, there is no possibility you don't know the answer to my question." Anto was very careful to make it a statement of fact. The Comte eyed him severely. After a moment of scrutiny, he responded.

"I have the answer to any question you may choose to ask Absolutely anything. And," he held up a finger, "I caution you. Do not test the boundaries of my rules like that again."

Anto gulped. He knew he was skirting the edge but had to press on.

"I am curious what you do with the...faces. There is nothing in the lore about it."

"Why, I add them to my collection, of course." With a grin, he pointed up. Anto raised his eyes. Above him, the ceiling was covered with disembodied faces, as if peeled from the victims only recently. Hundreds upon hundreds of vacant eyes stared down at him, mouths open. They were everywhere, hanging from every strut, pinned to every inch of the ceiling. Too many to count. And every one looked fresh. The skin was healthy and full, none were dried or shriveled. Lips and tongues pink and wet. Eyes reflecting the fire's light. It was as if they had just moments before been stripped from their bodies and hung overhead. If he didn't know better, he would have thought them macabre masks instead of actual faces from living people. As he stared in horror, he realized that eyes blinked, and mouths moved. They were alive, in a way. Anto felt his stomach turn and quickly lowered his gaze while the Comte chuckled.

"I move them, from time to time," the Comte said. "So they get a different view once in a while."

Anto closed his eyes and gave himself a moment to collect his thoughts. The Comte patiently waited, taking a sip from the cup on the table next to him and recrossing his legs.

"One last thing," Anto finally said. "It is said that there is a way to...regain my features."

"Oh, absolutely! It is rather simple. Honestly, I don't know why more customers don't make use of the policy. All that is required is that you directly utilize the information you receive. This, obviously, is a fairly broad statement but I assure you, I am quite lenient."

"How will—I mean, I assume there is a process..."

Again, the Comte gave him a hard look. "I will know. Now, I believe you have used up the last of my good graces. Are you prepared to ask your question?"

"I would like a moment yet."

"Of course." The Comte leaned back, steepling his fingers in front of his face. Anto felt like a cat was watching its prey. "You may make use of my sense rooms, if you wish."

Anto blinked. "Wh--I am not aware of what those are."

"Rooms dedicated to the senses, of course." Again, the pointy smile. "A room for taste, a room for sound and so on. I feel it is only far to give my customers one last opportunity to enjoy their facilities."

"That...that is very generous of you."

"Isn't it though?"

Anto could not imagine what those rooms would contain. He shook his head, focusing on his purpose.

"I think I shall pass on that."

"As you wish."

He closed his eyes, thinking of Ven. And then, for some reason, of Father. And Mother and Mum Gwinth, Mar and Jek. Although a large part of him tried to wallow in the horror and sorrow of his past, the love took the forefront. Love and determination. Now that he was here, across from the Face Stealer, he felt something close to relief. Gone were the doubts and fears. He had to do this. There was no turning back. Even while walking the path up the mountain, there had been a part of his mind that said, hypothetically, he could turn around, burst into flame and end it all. But that time had passed. He was going to ask his question. He was going to learn how to cure Ven.

And he was going to lose his face.

He swallowed the tears that were threatening to burst through and opened his eyes. He looked at the Comte Visage and nodded.

"A man I know has a strange illness. Oozing purple sores appear on his body and his strength wastes away. He has a fever yet is cool to the touch. I first encountered this disease in an older man but since then, I have learned it can strike someone of any age. It is fatal. The afflicted have about a year before succumbing. We have consulted every healer in the land. No one knows of a cure. Not even the fumes of a silver rose fire will cure it. Nothing known will."

"Silver rose fire? My, but you *are* determined, aren't you?"

Anto nodded silently.

"What is your question?"

"How do I cure this sickness?"

The Comte smiled broadly. Anto felt a movement in the air around him. The Comte leaned forward, reversed eyes boring into Anto.

"I know of this illness. The cure is actually quite simple. Feed the afflicted old bread with green mold and cover the sores with a balm made of the sap from the saw-leaf fern that grows on the snowy side of the oak. Do this for three days and he will recover."

Then, the Comte reached out his hand, long pale-yellow fingers spread wide. He snapped his hand closed and took Anto's world from him.

Nothingness.

Darkness.

No.
Not darkness.

Absence of light.

Of smells.

Of sound.

Absence of sense.

Nothingness.

Then

Panic.

Open your eyes!

No eyes to open.

Listen!

No ears to hear.

Scream!

No mouth to scream.

Anto reached up and felt his face. His lone remaining sense. Touch. Feel the skin where his nose once was. The depressions that once held his eyes.

Scream.

The scream was caged. A guttural noise from his throat. He felt the vibrations inside his chest.

A howl with nowhere to go.

As his brain tried to process the sudden loss of input, he shook. His muscles spasmed. An involuntary reaction to the trauma. His body slipped out of his control.

Anto felt something. Pressure on his shoulders. Pushing him. Then, cold on his skin. He shivered. A vibration. More vibrations. More pressure on his back. Pushing him forward, forcing him off-balance. He took a step, his foot landing heavily, unsure where he was going. How far it was to the ground. He stumbled. He threw his arms out as he fell. His knee hit something hard. His hands and shoulders jarred violently as he stopped. He collapsed. Something grainy on his cheek.

A sob convulsed his chest, kept contained within him. He reached forward, feeling dirt between his fingers. Was that a breeze on his skin? Outside then. He got his hands under his chest and pushed himself up, kneeling in the dirt. He felt the cold wind again. Definitely outside.

More vibrations.

Then, something touched his arm. Instinctively he pulled away. With no visual cues to guide him, he lost his balance and fell again, this time scraping his elbow, just barely avoiding breaking it. Again, he felt vibrations in the air around him.

Was that...talking?

Someone was talking to him!

The woman. The woman who had been waiting outside the chalet. She promised to help him.

He reached out. Then snatched his hand back.

Was it her?

What if she had left. Was it someone else? How could he be sure?

He felt vibrations. He knew there was someone next to him.

How could he know who it was?

The panic rose in his again. His mind struggled to stay rational, forced as it was to deal with a completely irrational situation.

Then, he felt something cool touch his hand. He instinctively pulled away, but the object touched him again. He curled his fingers around it and, with a deep sense of relief, realized it was his canteen. His canteen he had given the woman outside the chalet. Again, he felt vibrations. Soft. Near him but subtle. He held the canteen and nodded, not understanding her words but hoping she understood his gesture as a sign of trust.

Hands on his shoulders, turning him. Then the hands were gone. He felt warmth on the right side of his head. The sun?

Cautiously, he stepped forward, his foot coming down too hard, the ground coming up too fast. But after a few more tries, he had gained a better sense of how to walk without seeing the ground. Still, he shuffled more than walked. Even the smallest rock or shallowest dip painfully sent him to his knees. He slowly moved forward, keeping the warmth on his right, until he stumbled into a bush. Feeling around, he turned slightly, following the curving path. He tripped over a fallen log. Feeling around in the dirt, he grasped a long branch. He sat for a moment, stripping the branches. Then, regaining his feet, he swung it in front of him, hitting obstacles as he walked. He clung to that tiny anchor of the wood, his only connection to the unseen, unheard world around him. Swinging it back and forth, he connected with rocks and trees and stayed on the trail.

He tried to sing his songline but couldn't focus. His mind was too jumbled to concentrate. He remembered though that the trail just before the Comte's chalet was straight and true, so he kept walking. Slowly. Carefully. Trying to get his mind to focus. At one point, he felt a touch on his arm, and he swung the stick wildly, connecting with something. Vibrations, and then he was alone once more.

I need to think! He scolded himself. *I need to remember!*

The warmth of the sun gradually left him. He assumed it was night. It didn't matter. Onward he stumbled. His stomach grumbled. His throat was dry. The Face Stealer's curse kept him alive but didn't stop his body from wanting sustenance. He tried to ignore the discomfort, concentrating on moving, on putting a foot forward, testing with his stick, then another foot. Bit by bit. One moment after another. Trying not to think about his hunger, his thirst, his fear of what may be right next to him. He thought of Ven. He focused on his songline.

He kept moving.

The inability to express himself was driving him mad. He couldn't scream. He couldn't cry. Couldn't laugh or smile or arch an eyebrow. Everything he felt, every fear and worry, was caged inside him with no way out.

His only outlet was movement. He could punch. And kick. And dance. And if he was brave, he could run. His lone remaining sense was touch. He felt the rough bark of the oak. He let the cool water of the stream run over his hand. In his head, he sang his songline, thought of Ven, and stumbled forward by touching the unseen world around him. All the while, he kept his thoughts away from what he had lost. No, not lost. Given away. Sacrificed for his love. If only he could cure Ven, he would be whole again.

If only.

He was tired. So very, very tired. There was warmth again, this time behind him on his left. Dawn. He had been stumbling down the mountain all night. When his stick hit a large rock, he sat, resting his weary muscles. Once or twice, he felt the air around him shift, as if someone, or something, was moving past him. He couldn't help but flinch each time. He now lived in a world of unknown entities and pain, unable to give voice to his frustration.

But Ven was depending on him.

He got to his feet, ignoring the protests of his muscles. Swinging his stick in front of him, he cautiously continued down the mountain. The trail, he remembered, was a single, winding path. He knew he needed to stay on the trail and continue down. Once off the mountain, he only had a few days of walking to make it home.

A few days of stumbling blind and deaf through the countryside, guided only by the songline he sang and the need to save the man he loved.

Thoughts of Ven gave him strength. Strength to move his sore legs. To keep going. To ignore the protests of his body and soul. Eventually, the ground leveled out. He felt warmth on top of his head. The wind wasn't as biting. He had reached the foot of the mountain. His cheeks rose in a non-existent smile. One more obstacle overcome.

Time was an abstraction, a thing around the edge of his existence. He saw nothing but blackness, smelled nothing at all. The world spun around him, but he was trapped within his head, unable to experience it.

At times, he thought he was making progress. Other times, he wondered if he was walking in circles. He sang the songline to himself, hunting for the tree trunks or bridges from the verses. Once, he was sure he was on the right path only to run into a hedgerow that wasn't supposed to be there. Despairing, he backtracked to his last point of certainty and tried again, moving slower so as to not miss a turn. Again and again, he was forced to stop, retrace his steps, and try again.

At one point, he got so frustrated, he flailed in the underbrush, swinging his stick wildly and breaking it. He didn't realize it was broken until his rage was spent. It took a long time to find another branch and then backtrack to a spot where his songline could guide him once more.

All his efforts, though, were for nothing. His hope, his reason for continuing, came to an abrupt end.

He was singing, carefully following verse by verse, when suddenly something clamped onto his leg. Pain shot through his body, followed quickly by the terror of the unknown. He was knocked down and felt himself being dragged. It was pure luck that he managed to hold onto the stick. He struck, hitting something. The pain in his leg deepened, as if a wild creature was biting into his flesh. Panicking, Anto struck again and again. Thorns scratched his skin as he was dragged into the bush. He kicked with his free leg, hitting softness. The jagged daggers shook his leg, tearing muscle and skin. With his free hand, he tried to protect himself from the branches and thorns slicing him.

Desperate, he grabbed hold of the stick with both hands and brought it down with all his strength. The daggers released. He swung again, connecting with his attacker. A third swing hit nothing. He reached down, feeling his leg. It was wet with what he assumed was blood. Then the daggers returned, this time on his arm. Too close to use the stick, Anto dropped it and punched. He felt his fist bury into a furry body and the daggers let go once more.

He grabbed the stick and scrambled to his feet, waving it, turning in circles, hopelessly trying to keep the beast at bay. By chance, he hit it again, but only a glancing blow. Around and around, he spun on his good leg, barely keeping his balance. The stick hit something solid. Reaching out, he felt bark and immediately put his back against it. Tired and wounded, he kept swinging and praying. The stick hit nothing but air. The beast did not attack again. Whether it had left or was simply waiting him out, Anto had no idea. He stood there until his breathing slowed. His leg and arm burned with pain. His skin was cold with blood and sweat.

Slowly, he pushed away from the tree. His foot caught on a root and he stumbled forward. Images of fangs tearing out his throat filled his head, and he brought an arm up to cover his head and neck. He waited for teeth to sink into him, but they never came. Quickly, he regained his feet, sweeping the stick around him. Nothing. He took another step. Branches pushed against him, slicing thin cuts into his shins. Another step and again he fell. His hand landed hard, twisting his wrist painfully. He rolled, grabbing at it. His back hit water and he was immediately soaked.

Fighting through the pain, he dunked his injured leg in the water, letting the cool liquid wash away the blood and clean the wound. He tore his pants leg and wrapped it around the bite, stopping the bleeding. He did the same for his arm. He was running on instinct, knowing he needed to bind his wounds. He felt his body, trying to get an idea of how badly he was injured, doing the best he could.

Getting to his feet once more, he staggered forward, expecting death by razor sharp fangs with every step.

The small glimmer of hope that sparked at the thought the beast had decided he wasn't worth the trouble was quickly snuffed when he realized he had no idea which direction the road lay. He was in the bush, hopelessly turned around. Despair hit him and he crumbled to his knees in the water. Without the road, he had no hope of finding home. He was lost.

He had failed.

The anguish was overwhelming. He thought of Ven, slowly wasting away. He wondered if Mar would tell him the truth when he asked where his love had gone. Why he wasn't at his side. His body shook, needing a way to purge the emotions that consumed him. Unshod tears were drowning him. Unscreamed cries deafened him.

Suddenly, hands grabbed at him. Anto jumped away, crashing into a wall of thorns. He barely felt the thousand cuts as he fought this new assailant. Again and again, hands grabbed at him, holding him, pushing him. He swung his stick, feeling it connect solidly. But then it was yanked from his grasp. There were strong vibrations. He assumed the person was yelling. He voicelessly screamed back.

Leave me alone!

Left with only his hands, bloodied with broken fingernails, he clawed at the attacker. A sudden blow to the side of his head stunned him and he staggered into a tree. As he lurched forward, his arms were wrapped in rope. The rope was pulled taunt, pinning his arms to his sides.

Please! Just leave me alone! He cried inside.

Instead, he was yanked forward. He stumbled and the rope pulled him again. He had no choice but to follow. Unable to see, bereft of his stick, Anto struggled to make any progress as he was led through the brush. His captor kept the rope taunt. Bit by bit, he stumbled along, his despair deepening with each step. He was lost and now captured. There was nothing left for him to do but to give in.

He slid another foot forward. This time, instead of pushing through weeds or catching a root, it encountered nothing but dirt. Same with the next. They were back on the road.

Vibrations. His captor speaking. The rope slackened, and, although still tight around his body, at least he wasn't being pulled off balance. Anto waited for a moment and then leapt away. He took off in a blind sprint. Knowing he was foolish yet needing to try something, anything, he ran. The rope around his chest constricted violently and he was stopped dead in his tracks. The rope pulled again, taking him off his feet. He felt a rib crack when he landed in the dust.

More yelling over him. He expected to be beat, but no blows came. Instead, after a moment or two, strong hands lifted to his feet and pushed him forward. Once more, the lead slackened. This time, he felt the presence of something next to him. Something big. His chest was bumped. Not violently. Rather, it felt like...a horse. Another bump and he was sure. He was standing next to a horse.

Hands grabbed his leg, lifting it. There was another flare of defiance in Anto, but it almost immediately died. What was the point? He was going to be taken by this person, either upright or unconscious. Resigned, Anto allowed his captor to guide his foot to the stirrup. Once saddled, he was tied in place, preventing him from falling. Intentionally or not.

His captor set an easy pace. Without the stress of picking his way through the countryside, his thoughts turned inward.

When Anto was twenty years old:

"Come on! Hurry!"

"I'm coming!"

Ven grinned and reached down, grabbing Anto's hand and pulling him up the hill.

"What's the rush?"

"Just hurry!"

Together, they climbed the hill. They were in the countryside near Ven's family's farm. It was almost midnight. Above them, a million stars twinkled. The moon, almost full, provided them plenty of blue light to see by. As they neared the crown of the hill, Ven slowed. Anto looked around. From their vantage, they could see a large portion of the countryside. Endless fields, meandering rivers. Tiny points of light, scattered across the land, indicated farmhouses and, in the far distance, the cluster of a town.

"This way."

Ven grabbed his hand and pulled him forward. Hand in hand, they walked through the short, wind-swept grass. Before them, Anto spotted a low stone wall. It curved around the top of the hill, enclosing the crown.

They stopped a few paces from the wall.

"Are you ready?" Ven asked with a grin.

"I don't even know what we're doing out here," Anto replied. "How can I be ready?"

Ven's grin grew wider and, giving his hand a squeeze, led him to the wall. Looking over, Anto's breath caught in his throat.

Before them, protected by the wall, were a thousand flowers, blooming in the moonlight. As his mind tried to take in the scene, the wind shifted slightly, and the most wondrous scent touched his nose. Floral yet not passive, strong but not overwhelming, the scent wrapped around them, made them feel safe. Made them feel loved. The blossoms, deep velvety purple, four-petaled and hand-sized, were turned towards the moon.

"It's...it's incredible."

"They only bloom in the brightest of moonlight," Ven said, his voice low and respectful. "Their smell is said to be able to calm a raging bull ox."

"What are they called?"

"Lunagift."

"I've never heard of them before."

"They only grow in very special areas. Ma took me and Jek here where we were little a couple times."

"So beautiful."

Anto, dazzled by the sight, closed his eyes and breathed deep, filling his head with the amazing smell of the lunagift. He turned and kissed Ven.

"Thank you."

A smile. A sparkle in the eye.

Together, they stood and let the lunagift fill their senses.

When Anto was twenty-two years old:

He couldn't help but think of the slaver from years ago. It wasn't right. After so many years of struggling, he had ended up in the same spot as back then; taken by another to be sold for who knew what purpose.

What good was a Faceless to a slaver? He wondered. The answer was almost immediate. Entertainment. After all, he was useless as a laborer. No. His fate was sealed. His mind created scenario after scenario of what awaited him. Would he be thrown in an arena, forced to battle a never-ending parade of unseen combatants? Or dropped in a labyrinth, destined to wander forever for the entertainment of others?

There was no way of knowing how long he wallowed in such thoughts. For a time, he simply tried to remember that, somewhere, the sun was shining in the sky. It didn't matter. All that mattered was that he would spend the rest of his days knowing Ven died in pain. Without him at his side.

The air was cool on his skin when they halted. Anto waited and waited, not bothering to move. Finally, he was unstrapped from the saddle, guided down, moved past something hot—a campfire—and bound to a tree until the air began warming once more.

Twice more, he was put on a horse until night, then bound until dawn. He noticed he was becoming more sensitive to the changes in the air. Temperature. Humidity near a river. Even the direction a warm breeze came from. Why he cared, he didn't know. His mind had to think about something, he supposed. Otherwise, he would fall into a pit of memories, of failures that wouldn't stop haunting him.

When Anto was sixteen years old:

Father was quiet. He had not spoken in days. Not a single word as Mother lay in bed, writhing in pain from the sickness that was taking her. Anto pressed a cool cloth to her fevered head, whispering softly to her as he thrashed, locked in a fever dream.

At first, he would look up whenever Father entered the room, expecting him to help. Or bring medicine. Or say a kind word to his wife. But he would stand in the doorway, looking at her with an unreadable face, like he wasn't sure if he was disgusted or disappointed. Or both. After the first few times, Anto didn't bother looking to him and Father, in turn, didn't bother even looking in on her.

As he sat with her those long hours, he told her of his dreams. He told her that, once she was better, he would take her away to someplace far away. They would start a new life, one filled with happiness and love.

She never heard him. She was locked in a nightmare of pain and would never escape it.

In the end, he was almost glad it was over.

When Anto was twenty-two years old:

The next time they stopped, it was the middle of the day. It was hot, with little breeze. Anto felt vibrations around him and was brought down off the horse. His heart hammered in his chest. His mind raced. What was to become of him now?

A pull on the rope. He stumbled forward, his foot catching on something. Instantly, hands were there to catch him. Why? Was he at the lip of a pit, his captors not yet ready to throw him to the dreadfoxes?

Suddenly, the rope was loosened. His arms were freed. More vibrations. He raised his fists, not quite ready to surrender completely to fate. Maybe he could inflict just the tiniest bit of pain on his captors before he was cast into a worse hell than he was already in. Maybe he could cause some pain too.

An object latched onto his side. Before he could react, it scrambled up his torso. He felt sharp tiny nails pierce his skin as it moved up his body. It wrapped around his shoulders once, twice, three times before stopping. He felt a wet roughness on his cheek. Over and over.

He was being licked.

He knew that sensation.

He reached up, feeling a long, furry body.

Anto sank to his knees, hugging Telos. Crying tears that couldn't be shed.

He was home.

Telos wouldn't stop wriggling around him, licking and rubbing his face against Anto. Then he felt arms embrace him and he knew he was safe. Truly safe. He reached out, taking them into his arms, wishing he could see them, hear them. As horrible as it was to have no outlet for the rage and sorrow, having no way to express his love and thanks was even worse. But he felt their tears on his skin and their kisses as well. He felt their arms around him and Telos snuggling against him.

Finally, they separated, although there was always a hand on his arm or around his shoulder. They were letting him know he was not alone.

Ven? He cried without a mouth. *Is Ven still alive?* He only felt two sets of hands but Ven had already lost so much strength before he had set out to find the Face Stealer. The hands, he could only assume they belonged to Mar and Jek, helped him to his feet. They slowly and carefully led him. His foot hit wood. They gently lifted his foot. A step. And another. He was inside. The air cooled around him for a moment before heating up with a different heat than before. Closer. Immediate. Like a hearth.

They were leading him into the house. The air around him was warm. Pressure on his left shoulder, directing him. Then hands to stop him. Hands to lift his foot. More stairs. Carefully, they lead him up.

To Ven's room!

He almost tore from their grasp, falling onto the hard stairs in the process. They got him back up and led him. But he knew the way. Top of the stairs and to the right. Second door. A moment later, he was at Ven's bed. He felt the softness of a blanket. Reaching out, he felt a body under the blanket. He pulled his hand back, hesitating. To come this far, to go through so much. What if...

He touched the body. Pressed his palm down. The body was still. Even if he had a mouth, he would have held his breath. Then, he felt another hand cover his. Weak. But there. The chest rose and fell. Ven shifted under the blanket.

He was still alive.

Anto's shoulders sagged in relief. He felt his heart pound in his chest. There was still time.

He gripped Ven's hand tightly, willing his love and strength to flow into him. Ven's body shook with a cough, stirring Anto out of his relieved stupor. Reluctantly, he pushed away from the bed, helped by the others. All he wanted to do was hold him. But he couldn't. Not yet. There was still time, but how much? How weak was he? How close to death was his love? He needed to hold him. Oh, how he needed to hold him. But he forced himself away. Carefully, they led him out of the room and back down the stairs. Knowing the house, he reached out for the table near the kitchen and found a chair.

His heart and mind were in turmoil. Just moments ago, he thought he was condemned to an eternity of pain and torture. Now, there was chance, slim though it was, to save Ven and break the curse. He tried to calm his thoughts. In a perverse way, the lack of senses helped. There was nothing to distract him from concentrating. He was locked in a private hell, far, far away from the outside world.

He placed his hands on the table for a moment, knowing they were watching him. Somehow, he had to tell them how to cure Ven. But how? None of them knew the letters used by the priests and scribes. The only written language they had was the simple symbols of trading. He traced the symbol for bread on the table. He waited. There was no movement around him.

He traced it again.

And again.

Finally, he felt something placed in his hand. He felt the hard crust of a loaf. Nodding, he mimed eating it. He felt movement in the air around him and quickly grunted, stopping them. He knew the loaf was fresh. Mar would never feed her son moldy bread.

He shook from frustration. To be this close to saving Ven and failing? No! There had to be a way. But how?

How to convey knowledge with no facial expressions? No words? The only tools he still retained were his hands...

Hands.

Touch.

He reached out, placing his hands palms up on the table. After a moment, he felt a pair of hands grasp his. They were rough and bigger than his. He shook his head, pushed them aside and tried again. This time, smaller, finer hands touched his. He nodded. He flipped his hands over Mar's and assumed the starting position for negotiating at the Silent Market.

Anto could only imagine the look of surprise on Mar's face when she saw what he was doing. But she quickly took her position. Anto stretched both pinkies to touch hers, indicating the beginning of the silent dialog.

Bread.

Have bread.

Old. Bread.

Again.

Old. Bread. Old. Bread.

Again.

Anto shook his head in frustration. Mentally, he took a deep breath and closed his eyes. His insides vibrated from stress and he wanted nothing more than to let out a primal scream. Willing himself calm, he flexed his fingers and began again.

Old. Bread. Eat. Bad. Bread. Eat.

Eat. Bad. Bread.

Anto nodded.

No. Mar responded. *Bad. Bread. No good.*

He thumped his thumbs on the table, indicating he would not budge on his position.

Eat. Bad. Old. Bread. Three. Suns.

Mar hesitated, her left ring finger hovering over his, telling him she needed a moment to consider the offer. He felt vibrations. They were discussing his request. Finally, her finger lowered. She agreed.

More. Anto quickly slid his right pointer finger across her hand.

More.

White. Oak. Saw blade.

Again.

Saw blade. Oak. White.

He sensed vibrations. Talking.

Again.

Plant. Saw blade. Oak.

More vibrations.

Plant. Oak. Saw blade.

He nodded, praying they were understanding.

Then her ring finger touched his in agreement.

But he wasn't done yet.

Me. Me. Do.

Agreement.

Will acquire.

Anto nodded and sat back, not daring to hope. Not yet.

He fed the moldy bread, piece by piece, to Ven. His hands, bloodied by the razor-sharp edges of the saw fern leaves, gently spread the sap over every sore he could feel. At one point, he reached up to touch Ven's face and discovered a cloth over his eyes. He hoped Mar had covered them to save him the horror of seeing Anto's featureless head. He never left Ven's side. He wouldn't. Not again. Not ever. He was determined to stay there until Ven got better or...or he didn't. He couldn't see or hear him, but he could feel him, although the thin, bony body under his fingers wasn't the man he knew. Mar and Jek brought him more bread and ferns as he needed, plus warm water and cloth to wash Ven's wounds and cool ale for him to sip. Telos split his time between curled up in Anto's lap and, presumably, Ven's bed. The quipen wouldn't leave them, just as Anto wouldn't leave Ven.

Anto couldn't tell if his love was getting better. He didn't know how long the treatment would take. Or even if he had the correct ingredients. All he knew was that Ven was next to him. He could feel him, if nothing else. He questioned Mar, over and over.

Bad bread. Saw blade.

Yes. Bad bread. Old bread. Saw blade. Oak.

He had no choice to but trust in them. His hands trembled from the stress and worry. He didn't even care anymore that he couldn't see or hear or taste or smell. None of that mattered. Only Ven. If he spent the rest of his days trapped in his own head, so be it.

He just wanted Ven to get better.

Waiting at his bedside, Anto's thoughts again turned inward. Memories of watching the countryside roll past from Mum Gwinth's wagon. The smell of a campfire. Listening to the birds as he walked through the woods. His mind's eye was so focused on those times that he didn't, at first, realize the blackness of his world had subtly changed. The darkness was not quite as deep. And at the very moment he realized he once more had eyes to open, he heard for the first time in an eternity.

"Anto?"

Suddenly, sensations rushed through him, overwhelming and beautiful. Sobs burst from a throat no longer dead-ended. Tears finally flowed out of eyes that squinted open. He heard everything at once; the birds outside, the creak of the bed, Mar moving about downstairs. He smelled the meal being prepared and the sour sweat in the room.

And, as he blinked past the light and tears, he saw Ven.

Gaunt and pale though he was, he was alive and managed a small smile.

"Hey." His voice was thin and weak and the most beautiful thing Anto had ever heard.

"Hi," Anto croaked, finding a voice that he thought he had lost forever.

"You look terrible," Ven said.

He may have said something else, but the words didn't register because for the next several moments, Anto could do nothing but hug him and cry.

By nightfall, Ven had already regained enough strength to leave the bed with Anto's help. For the first time in a very long time, the five of them sat around the table and enjoyed Mar's cooking.

"I don't understand," Anto said between slow bites. He was determined to savor every morsel. "How did you find me?"

"I trailed you, from the moment you left," Jek said simply. "Ma's idea."

Mar smiled and patted Jek's arm. "I told him to keep his distance and never, under any circumstances, approach the mountain too closely."

"I was about half a day behind you," Jek admitted. "For a while, I thought I'd lost you. Actually, it was your fight with the dreadfox that caught my attention. The ruckus led me right to you."

"So you killed the dreadfox?"

Jek nodded.

"Did it do that?" Anto pointed to the large bruise on the side of his head.

"Oh no. That was all you," he laughed lightly. "Sorry I had to knock you down, but you weren't being cooperative."

"I didn't know." Anto felt his cheeks redden but Jek shrugged.

"No way you could have."

Anto fed Telos, who was purring in his lap, a piece of beef. "I...thank you."

"No," Mar shook her head. "We can't thank you enough. You brought Ven back to us."

"I still can't believe you did that," Ven said, his voice hard yet full. "You gambled everything."

Anto reached over and took Ven's hand into his. "I had to. I couldn't just sit around and watch you go."

Between bites, Anto and Ven got lost in each other's eyes all over again.

Later, Anto was outside, breathing in the night scents, trying not to think about his ordeal but having no success. He was sitting on a hill behind the house. Ven had gone to bed. Anto couldn't wait to wrap his arms around him and fall asleep to his heartbeat, just like they used to do. But he needed to clear his thoughts first. And he couldn't bring himself to close his eyes. Not quite yet. He needed to smell the night air and watch the flame beetles. He tried to absorb every scent and sight, taking nothing for granted.

"That was clever," a familiar voice spoke from the darkness.

Anto didn't have to turn to know who was behind him.

"Comte."

The yellow, angular broker of information and dispenser of curses stepped into view, hands in well-tailored pockets. "Very clever, using the language of the Silent Market. No one has thought of that before."

"Wasn't sure it was going to work," Anto admitted. "Mum Gwinth always said I was terrible at negotiating at market. Said my hands had a funny accent." He smiled at the memory.

The Comte Visage grunted. Despite his cool manner, Anto got the distinct impression the demon was unhappy about Anto breaking the curse.

"You will, of course, not tell anyone how you did it."

Anto shrugged. Maybe he was still euphoric at regaining his life, but he felt like challenging the demon. "Maybe."

The Comte shook his pointy head. "I don't think you understand. You are not able to convey the information. I have removed the ability from your mind. And from the minds of everyone involved."

"You can't do that!"

"My dear boy, I can take your entire face away with the snatch of my hand." The Comte reached out into the air and snapped his long fingers to emphasize the point. "Taking your memory is simplicity in itself."

"You don't want your business to suffer," Anto spat.

"Of course not. If word got out there was such an easy way out of the contract, I'd lose my entire enterprise."

"Would that be so bad? Why can't you help people instead of taking so much from them?"

The Comte laughed. It was not a pleasant laugh. "Knowledge has a price. If it didn't, everyone would have it. Trust me, that way lies madness."

"I don't trust you."

"Very wise. Wisdom too comes at a price. You've paid for your wisdom. Let others do the same."

"I'll have nightmares for the rest of my days."

The Comte nodded. "And yet you will wake each morning and forget those nightmares for a time. Until the darkness claims you for good."

Anto opened his mouth to respond but the Comte Visage was gone, leaving him alone in the night.

He smiled, despite the chill that followed the demon. Yes, he would have nightmares. For the remainder of his days. But he would wake from them. And feel Ven holding him. He would hear Ven's voice. He would speak and taste and smell. As a child, he had been overlooked. Ignored. He had been, in a way, just as faceless then.

Now, finally, he was seen. Heard.

Loved.

Faceless no more.

When Anto was twenty-five years old:

The fire wasn't the brightest Creekslope had ever seen, but it was the biggest. People from across the countryside came to give their blessings. To celebrate two lives becoming one. Although they had only been a part of the town for a few years, everyone shed rivers of joyful tears.

Standing in front of their neighbors, with Mar and Jek at their sides, Anto and Ven wrapped the cord around their intertwined hands. The ceremony was mostly for Mar's benefit. She deserved to see her youngest son, recovering and getting stronger by the day, be happy and laughing. And there was plenty of laughing. And dancing. The party lasted well into the night. At some point, Anto and Ven snuck away, hand in hand, into the surrounding countryside. While Telos patrolled the area for grubs, they sat, side by side, Ven's head on Anto's shoulder, and let the world spin past.

About the Author

Armed with little more than a lifted eyebrow and a sarcastic quip, JEFF MONDAY wanders the space between what you didn't say and what you sorta meant, listening to your tall tales and scribbling them down on the backs of cocktail napkins.

Look him up on the interweb at JeffMonday.net. Or buy him a drink at the pub. He's thirsty.

Printed in Great Britain
by Amazon

12426527R00121